SILVER BULLET

SILVER BULLET

by
Stephen King

Includes Stephen King's *Cycle of the Werewolf,*
the complete *Silver Bullet* screenplay,
and a new Foreword by the author

Illustrations by Bernie Wrightson

A SIGNET BOOK

NEW AMERICAN LIBRARY

*In memory of Davis Grubb,
and all the voices of Glory.*

NAL BOOKS ARE AVAILABLE AT QUANTITY DISCOUNTS WHEN USED
TO PROMOTE PRODUCTS OR SERVICES. FOR INFORMATION PLEASE WRITE
TO PREMIUM MARKETING DIVISION, NEW AMERICAN LIBRARY,
1633 BROADWAY, NEW YORK, NEW YORK 10019.

Cycle of the Werewolf was published by arrangement
with The Land of Enchantment and Stephen King.
It appeared previously in a limited hardcover edition
and is available as a Signet Special.

SIGNET, SIGNET CLASSIC, MENTOR, PLUME, MERIDIAN
and NAL BOOKS are published by New American Library,
1633 Broadway, New York, New York 10019

First Printing, October, 1985

1 2 3 4 5 6 7 8 9

PRINTED IN THE UNITED STATES OF AMERICA

Contents

Foreword

Silver Bullet is probably the only movie ever made that began as a calendar proposal. The proposal was made to me in the lobby of a hotel in Providence, Rhode Island, during the World Fantasy Convention in 1979, by a young man from Michigan named Christopher Zavisa. One of the reasons I agreed at least to consider Zavisa's proposal was that I was drunk. While drunk I would seriously consider a proposal that I buy the Brooklyn Bridge and have it moved to my backyard in Maine by U-Haul trailer. But that wasn't the only reason; there were two others.

First, and probably of lesser importance, Zavisa had an interesting concept. He thought maybe I could conceive a story which would run in twelve monthly installments of vignette length; each of these installments would be accompanied by a Berni Wrightson painting. I thought I had seen every kind of calendar imaginable—trivia calendars, calendars which spotlight the birthdays of famous writers, calendars which showcase the admirably showcasable body of Christie Brinkley, rock-and-roll calendars, recipe calendars—but a *story* calendar? That was a new one, at least to me. I started to play with it a little, to rock and roll with it a little, to see if there was anything there, and if there was, if I could make it work.

Second, Zavisa had approached me at exactly the right time and place; psychologically speaking, there could not have been a more opportune moment. He and I were in Providence along with five or six hundred others with an interest in things macabre and fantastical as attendees of the World Fantasy Convention. This is a Halloween-weekend get-together which has been an annual event in the writing community for the last ten years or so.

I had attended only one WFC before the one in Providence, and I went feeling both awed and rather guilty. I was, after all, rubbing elbows with writers I had idolized as a kid, writers who had taught me much of what I knew about my craft— guys like Robert Bloch, author of *Psycho*, Fritz Leiber, author of *Conjure Wife* and *Night's Black Agents*, Frank Belknap Long, author of *The Hounds of Tindalos*. And although forty years dead, Howard Phillips Lovecraft was very much present in spirit— Lovecraft, who had turned Providence and Central Falls and the little Massachusetts towns just to the east into a shadow-haunted wonderland in the magic stories he published in *Weird Tales* during the thirties.

My awe, then, should be fairly understandable. I think the reason for my sense of guilt should be pretty clear, too. Frank Belknap Long had come up to the convention from New York on a Greyhound bus because, at the age of eighty-two, he could not afford a train ticket, let alone a plane ticket. Bob Bloch and Fritz Leiber are both in comfortable circumstances—have no fear, this is not an introduction to *The Poor Little Match Girl* or *Nell over the Ice*—but neither they nor most of the writers I idolized (and was, in many cases, meeting for the first time) had ever enjoyed *in a lifetime* the success I had enjoyed since the publication of my first novel, *Carrie*. This was not because I was a better writer; it was because I was born in time to take perfect advantage of the shockwave of reader interest in tales of science fiction and the supernatural which has washed over the best-seller lists since the late 1970s. They had labored long and honorably in the pulp jungles; I came bopping along twenty years after the demise of *Weird Tales*, the most important of them, and simply reaped the bountiful harvest they had sown in that jungle.

I went braced—as I had the year before at the WFC in Fort Worth—to hear a lot of "Who's this young whippersnapper?"

comments, to endure a certain number of sniffs and snubs over my vampire novel, my haunted-hotel novel, my precognition novel. Such a reception would have been a little embarrassing, but in a way something of a relief. Little Stevie King does penance, if you see what I mean. Can somebody give me hallelujah. The kind and generous treatment I received instead from men I could still hardly dare think of as my colleagues relieved my mind but made me feel guiltier than ever.

So, in comes Chris Zavisa at a moment when I am (a) drunk and (b) as ready as I will ever be to do something *small*, something which will show I am a regular guy and (drumroll and flourish of coronets, please) NOT JUST IN IT FOR THE MONEY.

I told Chris I thought maybe we could work something out and went off to my room, hearing the voice of my mother echoing dolefully in my head: "If you were a girl, Stephen, you'd always be pregnant."

I went to sleep that night musing on the cyclic nature of the calendar, and by noon the next day something had suggested itself—probably the *only* something which fits so neatly into the format Zavisa was suggesting. That something, of course, was the werewolf myth. Show me twelve months, I'll show you twelve full moons. Twelve opportunities for the werewolf to appear and play hob with the locals of . . . well, call it Tarker's Mills.

Chris liked it (although in all honesty I must tell you that in his eagerness to "marry" Berni Wrightson and me, I think he would have liked *Godzilla vs. the Stay-Puft Marshmallow Man*). I told him I'd give it a go, and by the time I got home I'd worked out a plan of attack—or a theme, if you like that better—that amused me. Call it *The Wolfman in Winesburg, Ohio*. I thought I could key in the full-moon motif to all sorts of holidays. My wife, Tabby, reminded me that a year where all the full moons fell on holidays would be a mad year indeed. I agreed, but invoked creative license. "I think your license should be revoked for speeding, dear," she said, and wandered off to make us all something to eat.

What worried me a lot more than full-moon holidays was the calendar motif. Even given five hundred words per install-

9

ment—a lot for a single calendar double spread which would already include a Wrightson painting and a month grid—I was going to be cutting it very close to the bone. I didn't like the idea of telling the story in "See Dick, See Jane, See Dick and Jane" terms, but I didn't see any way around it.

I sat down to the typewriter, determined to knock one off a day and finish in twelve days. I did January, February, and March, and then a set of galleys came in that had to be corrected and returned immediately. I set *Cycle of the Werewolf* aside to do the galleys and didn't get back to it for four months. Every now and then I would look guiltily at the thin sheaf of pages gathering dust beside the typewriter, but look was all I did. It was a cold meal. Nobody likes to eat a cold meal unless he has to.

Chris Zavisa was a paragon of patience, but he finally gave me a call in January of 1981 and asked me how it was going. Guilt rushed over me anew. I had promised, and looky here— I was welshing. Lying through my teeth, I told Chris it was coming along real well. He brightened at once. That was good, he said, because Berni Wrightson had already commenced on the preliminary sketches.

We left *en famille* for a two-week vacation in Puerto Rico about three weeks after that call, and I took the first three months of *Cycle* with me, determined to be a professional, bite the bullet, and finish the thing off.

I did April on the airplane. I was just finishing when the No Smoking sign came on and the plane, then over the Atlantic, banked sharply back toward New York. A man had suffered a heart attack—the No Smoking signs were lit because he was getting oxygen.

On our second try at the New York–to–San Juan leg, I finished May. We arrived in San Juan without incident this time, but there was some sort of a hold-up on the station wagon we'd rented from Avis (with three kids I *always* rent a wagon; a big thyroidal Country Squire if I can get it), and while we were sitting in the Avis office and sweating into our touristy clothes, I did June.

Man, I'm flying on this sucker, I thought. Gimme a traffic

jam between here and Palmas del Mar and I'll be all the way to fall!

Nothing like that happened, though, and the manuscript simply sat on a table in the little beachside cottage we'd taken for the next week while we drank in the sun, sipped piña coladas, slept in the afternoon, and generally tried to forget what Maine's like in the blue heart of February. I was also trying grimly to quit smoking—when they wheeled the unfortunate heart attack victim down the center aisle of the plane with the plastic mask over his face, I had clearly seen the pack of Marlboros in his breast pocket.

Along about the start of the second week, the manuscript of *Cycle* sent up a very thin cry from the occasional table where I had dropped it when we first came into the cottage . . . the table where it still remained.

You know that cry when you hear it; you always know. It is, I think, very much like the cry of a blue baby who is at first taken for dead. *Please, I'd like to try to live, if you don't mind too awfully much,* that cry says.

And if I'm going to be dead honest with you, I've got to say that I thought *Cycle of the Werewolf* was a stillbirth. Half of it was done, true enough, and the other half *would* be done— barring fire, flood, heart attack, or plane crash, I had no doubt of that—because I had promised, and I would much rather do bad work than break my word. But nothing was happening. The first six months had been like six yanks on the pull cord of a lawnmower that's got an empty gas tank. The vignette form was killing me. I felt like something that has been bent, folded, stapled, and mutilated.

But . . . I could hear it crying, just the same.

I took my notebook and sat down at the kitchenette table, brushing away the sugar my kids had spilled while loading up their Wheaties at breakfast. And I started to write about this kid named Marty, who was stuck in a wheelchair, and how burned he was because the werewolf had not been content with just killing people; now the werewolf had managed to get the big Fourth of July fireworks show cancelled.

The installment spilled far over the arbitrary five-hundred-word limit I had imposed on myself, but I didn't care. I was excited, almost feverish. And what happens at the best times happened then: I could see ahead of what I was writing to all the things I *would* write, and I could see backward to all the things I would fix up. It's like feeling around in the dark and finally finding the light switch just as you were about to give up. That's the best I can describe it.

By the time we went back to Maine, I had finished July, August, and September. One of the first things I did after getting back to work was pick up the phone and call Chris Zavisa—I did it as soon as possible because it's best to get distasteful things over with as quickly as possible, and telling Chris that his calendar had become a sort of twelve-part novella was not a thing I wanted to do.

But I was as wrong about Zavisa's reaction as I had been about the sort of response I expected to receive at the World Fantasy Convention. Instead of being angry or depressed, he was delighted. We could do a slim book instead of a calendar, he said . . . and he said it with such real enthusiasm that I wondered if it wasn't what he had sort of wanted all along, but had been, maybe, a little too shy to pitch.

At any rate, the manuscript was finished in another two weeks, and published in a limited edition in 1983. That edition, done by Chris Zavisa's Land of Enchantment Press, has now sold out. I had not intended that it should be reprinted—one of the ways I've tried to keep my own career in perspective is to try, from time to time, to find alternative ways to publish, to get out from under the sheer weight of numbers. *Cycle* was such a case. But the best-laid plans of mice and men, as Robert Burns once observed, gang oft agley. Whatever *that* means.

In this case I think it means Dino DeLaurentiis came along.

II

Although he probably stands no more than five-six or five-seven, Dino DeLaurentiis is one of the biggest men I have ever known. He is a man for whom the word *style* seems to have been invented; a man of poise, charm, persuasiveness, *panache*. And he is *very* fond of the grand gesture.

After buying the rights to make *The Dead Zone,* Dino flew up to Bangor in a Learjet to pitch me on the idea of writing the screenplay. Man, when the gas jockeys at the civil air terminal saw that Lear come cruising up, they just about fell down and genuflected.

I met Dino and drove him home, not sure what to say or how to behave; while the quality of his films has varied wildly from the sublime (*Two Women*) to the ridiculous (*Amityville 3-D*), he is surely one of the greatest producers in the world and probably *the* greatest now living . . . and he was in *my* car.

"Stephen," he said, lighting a cigarette and looking out at the mostly uninteresting snowscape of Outer Hammond Street on a February afternoon, "this is Bangor, Maine . . . right?"

"Right," I said.

"Is in New Hampshire, right?"

"Right," I said. It was all I could think of.

Dino charmed me; he charmed my wife; he charmed my children. He charmed us all in spite of the fact that the pain from some severely abscessed teeth was nearly killing him (he flew to Rome the following day to have them attended to— the phrase *here today, gone tomorrow* was also made for Dino). I agreed to write the screenplay; he agreed at least to sound out Bill Murray's agent on the possibility of having Murray, who was my choice for Johnny Smith, in the picture.

As it happened, none of it worked out. My screenplay was rejected in favor of one by Jeffery Boam, and Chris Walken ended up playing Johnny Smith. No matter; it turned out to be a pretty damned good picture anyway.

In the two years which followed, Dino bought a lot of my stuff. The results have varied—I was not wild about *Firestarter*— but on the whole they have been pretty good. And along the way I have found he is a man I can always count on as a man. He is businesslike, but he is honest and generous, as well.

I've never asked him why he has bought so many things of mine for films, but I think it may be because we share many of the same interests: an urge to entertain people; a rather childish interest in the largeness of effect; the idea that simple stories may be the best ones; a sentimental belief that most people are good and that, in general, cowardice tends to be a scarcer commodity than bravery when the chips are down.

Whatever the reasons, he has on several occasions asked if I had anything else he might like, and I have found myself going looking—not just because he pays well (although he does) or because he actually makes the movies he says he's going to make (although he does that, too) but because I like working with him, and I'm always interested to see what he's going to do next. Working with Dino is a little like running away to be in the circus.

In early 1984 I happened to think of *Cycle of the Werewolf,* and sent him a copy. I didn't really expect him to be interested; it was a little courtesy gesture, no more. I certainly didn't think he or anyone else would be interested in making a werewolf movie, especially after *The Howling, An American Werewolf in Paris,* and *Wolfen*—all three really excellent movies (at least in Yr. Correspondent's humble opinion) and not a solid financial success among them. But Dino did, and a week later we had come to terms.

I expected that my involvement with the film would end with signing my name on the dotted line, but that wasn't the way it worked out—as things now stand, I have written three movies for Dino, am scheduled to direct the third of those, and didn't mean to have anything to do with any of them.

One of the things which amuses and interests me about Dino is how successful he has been in getting me to do things I had no intention of doing. He bought a number of my *Night Shift* short stories from American/British producer Milton Subotsky and asked me if I would write an original story to go with two of the stories he already had. I had a story in mind called "Cat's Eye" that was supposed to be about a little boy whose cat is falsely accused of trying to kill him by stealing his breath. I switched the sex (Dino wanted Drew Barrymore, who was then shooting *Firestarter,* to play the part of the child) and turned the story into a little film script.

Dino came up to Bangor in his Lear again, this time accompanied by Martha Schumacher, the film's producer, and sat in my office and drank coffee and somehow persuaded me to write the whole script. I'm still not entirely sure how he did it; I think it was a form of benign hypnotism. I started by shaking my head and saying it absolutely couldn't be done, my schedule was killing me already, and ended by nodding the fool thing and telling him I could have a first-draft screenplay for him in a month or so.

About a week after the *Cycle of the Werewolf* deal was signed, I was in New York. I stopped in Dino's office—which has the city's most stupefyingly beautiful view of Central Park, I think—just to say hello. Dino asked me if I'd consider doing a script for *Cycle.* I told him it was impossible, my schedule was killing me, etc., etc., etc.

About a week after that, back in Maine again, I happened to have the house to myself on an overcast Sunday afternoon. Lying on the sofa with the Sunday paper beside me, I was flicking through the TV channels and happened on *To Kill a Mockingbird,* a movie I hadn't seen since I saw it in first run (or whatever passes for first run up here in the boonies) at the Cumberland Theater in Brunswick, Maine—and at that time I must have been all of eleven.

I found myself first absorbed by those grainy black-and-white images, and then almost transported. When it ended I actually cried a little—it was the voice of the girl, mostly, recalling those events which were playing themselves out before my eyes. I turned off the TV and thought: What would happen if you tried to use that elegiac, retrospective, and rather gentle form of narration to tell the story of Marty Coslaw and his duel with the werewolf?

The idea excited me—it was like finding that light switch again, this time without even having to grope for it. Twenty minutes after the movie was over I was walking around the house, thinking about how it could work, snapping my fingers with excitement. I called Dino the next day and said I would try it if he still wanted me. He said he did, and I wrote the screenplay which follows.

To direct the picture, Dino hired a young, amiable, fiercely bright Californian named Dan Attias. *Silver Bullet* is his first feature. Dan and I worked hard on it, he giving a little here, I giving a little there. I think that things turned out as well as they ever do when you're spending ten to twelve million dollars on a piece of make-believe: we compromised when we had to and all ended up still friends.

I like the screenplay a lot, and that's why I've allowed it to be reprinted here. Is the picture any good? Man, I just can't tell. I'm writing without benefit of hindsight and from a deeply subjective point of view. You want that point of view? Okay. I think it's either very good indeed or a complete bust. Past a certain point you simply can't tell (and probably my punishment will turn out to be just this: in ten years no one will remember it at all, one way or the other). After you've been through four drafts plus spot rewrites, the film itself seems like a hallucination when you first see it.

Two things I *am* sure of: Megan Follows, who plays Jane Coslaw, is probably going to be a star. And I'd like to have that rocket sled of a wheelchair.

That's enough of the background; the dreams are ahead. Enjoy yourself, and as always, thanks for checking in with me.

—Stephen King

Bangor, Maine
February 12, 1985

CYCLE OF THE WEREWOLF

In the stinking darkness under the barn, he raised his shaggy head. His yellow, stupid eyes gleamed. *"I hunger,"* he whispered.

Henry Ellender
The Wolf

Thirty days hath September
April, June, and November,
all the rest but the Second have thirty-one,
Rain and snow and jolly sun,
and the moon grows fat in every one.

Child's rime

JANUARY
FEBRUARY
MARCH
APRIL
MAY
JUNE
JULY
AUGUST
SEPTEMBER
OCTOBER
NOVEMBER
DECEMBER

Somewhere, high above, the moon shines down, fat and full—but here, in Tarker's Mills, a January blizzard has choked the sky with snow. The wind rams full force down a deserted Center Avenue; the orange town plows have given up long since.

Arnie Westrum, flagman on the GS&WM Railroad, has been caught in the small tool-and-signal shack nine miles out of town; with his small, gasoline-powered rail-rider blocked by drifts, he is waiting out the storm there, playing Last Man Out solitaire with a pack of greasy Bicycle cards. Outside the wind rises to a shrill scream. Westrum raises his head uneasily, and then looks back down at his game again. It is only the wind, after all...

But the wind doesn't scratch at doors... and whine to be let in.

He gets up, a tall, lanky man in a wool jacket and railroad coveralls, a Camel cigarette jutting from one corner of his mouth, his seamed New England face lit in soft orange tones by the kerosene lantern which hangs on the wall.

The scratching comes again. Someone's dog, he thinks, lost and wanting to be let in. That's all it is... but still, he pauses. It would be inhuman to leave it out there in the cold, he thinks (not that it is much warmer in here; in spite of the battery-powered heater, he can see the cold cloud of his breath)—but still he hesitates. A cold finger of fear is probing just below his heart. This has been a bad season in Tarker's Mills; there have been omens of evil on the land. Arnie has his father's Welsh blood strong in his veins, and he doesn't like the feel of things.

Before he can decide what to do about his visitor, the low-pitched whining rises to a snarl. There is a thud as something incredibly heavy hits the door... draws back... hits again. The door trembles in its frame, and a puff of snow billows in from the top.

Arnie Westrum stares around, looking for something to shore it up with, but before he can do more than reach for the flimsy chair he has been sitting in, the snarling thing strikes the door again with incredible force, splintering it from top to bottom.

It holds for a moment longer, bowed in on a vertical line, and lodged in it, kicking and lunging, its snout wrinkled back in a snarl, its yellow eyes blazing, is the biggest wolf Arnie has ever seen . . .

And its snarls sound terribly like human words.

The door splinters, groans, gives. In a moment the thing will be inside.

In the corner, amongst a welter of tools, a pick leans against the wall. Arnie lunges for it and seizes it as the wolf thrusts its way inside and crouches, its yellow eyes gleaming at the cornered man. Its ears are flattened back, furry triangles. Its tongue lolls. Behind it, snow gusts in through a door that has been shattered down the center.

It springs with a snarl, and Arnie Westrum swings the pick.

Once.

Outside, the feeble lamplight shines raggedly on the snow through the splintered door.

The wind whoops and howls.

The screams begin.

Something inhuman has come to Tarker's Mills, as unseen as the full moon riding the night sky high above. It is the Werewolf, and there is no more reason for its coming now than there would be for the arrival of cancer, or a psychotic with murder on his mind, or a killer tornado. Its time is now, its place is here, in this little Maine town where baked bean church suppers are a weekly event, where small boys and girls still bring apples to their teachers, where the Nature Outings of the Senior Citizens' Club are religiously reported in the weekly paper. Next week there will be news of a darker variety.

Outside, its tracks begin to fill up with snow, and the shriek

of the wind seems savage with pleasure. There is nothing of God or Light in that heartless sound—it is all black winter and dark ice.

The cycle of the Werewolf has begun.

JANUARY
FEBRUARY
MARCH
APRIL
MAY
JUNE
JULY
AUGUST
SEPTEMBER
OCTOBER
NOVEMBER
DECEMBER

Love, Stella Randolph thinks, lying in her narrow virgin's bed, and through her window streams the cold blue light of a St. Valentine's Day full moon.

Oh love love love, love would be like—

This year Stella Randolph, who runs the Tarker's Mills Set 'n Sew, has received twenty Valentines—one from Paul Newman, one from Robert Redford, one from John Travolta . . . even one from Ace Frehley of the rock group Kiss. They stand open on the bureau across the room from her, illuminated in the moon's cold blue light. She sent them all to herself, this year as every year.

Love would be like a kiss at dawn . . . or the last kiss, the real one, at the end of the Harlequin romance stories . . . love would be like roses in twilight . . .

They laugh at her in Tarker's Mills, yes, you bet. Small boys joke and snigger at her from behind their hands (and sometimes, if they are safe across the street and Constable Neary isn't around, they will chant *Fatty-Fatty-Two-By-Four* in their sweet, high mocking sopranos), but she knows about love, and about the moon. Her store is failing by inches, and she weighs too much, but now, on this night of dreams with the moon a bitter blue flood through frost-traced windows, it seems to her that love is still a possibility, love and the scent of summer as *he* comes . . .

Love would be like the rough feel of a man's cheek, that rub and scratch—

And suddenly there is a scratching at the window.

She starts up on her elbows, the coverlet falling away from her ample bosom. The moonlight has been blocked out by a dark shape—amorphous but clearly masculine, and she thinks: *I am dreaming . . . and in my dreams, I will let him come . . . in my dreams I will let myself come. They use the word dirty, but the word is clean, the word is right; love would be like coming.*

She rises, convinced that this is a dream, because there *is* a

31

man crouched out there, a man she *knows,* a man she passes on the street nearly everyday. It is—

(love love is coming, love has come)

But as her pudgy fingers fall on the cold sash of the window she sees it is not a man at all; it is an animal out there, a huge, shaggy wolf, his forepaws on the outer sill, his rear legs buried up to the haunches in the snowdrift which crouches against the west side of her house, here on the outskirts of town.

But it's Valentine's day and there will be love, she thinks; her eyes have deceived her even in her dream. It is a man, *that* man, and he is so wickedly handsome.

(wickedness yes love would be like wickedness)

and he has come this moon-decked night and he will take her. He will—

She throws the window up and it is the blast of cold air billowing her filmy blue nightgown out behind that tells her that *this is no dream.* The man is gone and with a sensation like swooning she realizes he was never there. She takes a shuddering, groping step backward and the wolf leaps smoothly into her room and shakes itself, spraying a dreamy sugarpuff of snow in the darkness.

But love! Love is like . . . is like . . . like a scream—

Too late she remembers Arnie Westrum, torn apart in the railroad shack to the west of town only a month before. Too late . . .

The wolf pads toward her, yellow eyes gleaming with cool lust. Stella Randolph backs slowly toward her narrow virgin's bed until the back of her pudgy knees strike the frame and she collapses upon it.

Moonlight parts the beast's shaggy fur in a silvery streak.

On the bureau the Valentine cards shiver minutely in the

breeze from the open window; one of them falls and seesaws lazily to the floor, cutting the air in big silent arcs.

The wolf puts its paw up on the bed, one on either side of her, and she can smell its breath...hot, but somehow not unpleasant. Its yellow eyes stare into her.

"Lover," she whispers, and closes her eyes.

It falls upon her.

Love is like dying.

JANUARY
FEBRUARY
MARCH
APRIL
MAY
JUNE
JULY
AUGUST
SEPTEMBER
OCTOBER
NOVEMBER
DECEMBER

MARCH

WRIGHTSON 1983

The last real blizzard of the year—heavy, wet snow turning to sleet as dusk comes on and the night closes in—has brought branches tumbling down all over Tarker's Mills with the heavy gunshot cracks of rotted wood. Mother Nature's pruning out her deadwood, Milt Sturmfuller, the town librarian, tells his wife over coffee. He is a thin man with a narrow head and pale blue eyes, and he has kept his pretty, silent wife in a bondage of terror for twelve years now. There are a few who suspect the truth—Constable Neary's wife Joan is one—but the town can be a dark place, and no one knows for sure but them. The town keeps its secrets.

Milt likes his phrase so well that he says it again: Yep, Mother Nature is pruning her deadwood . . . and then the lights go out and Donna Lee Sturmfuller utters a gasping little scream. She also spills her coffee.

You clean that up, her husband says coldly. You clean that up right . . . now.

Yes, honey. Okay.

In the dark, she fumbles for a dishtowel with which to clean up the spilled coffee and barks her shin on a footstool. She cries out. In the dark, her husband laughs heartily. He finds his wife's pain more amusing than anything, except maybe the jokes they have in The Reader's Digest. Those jokes—Humor in Uniform, Life in These United States—really tickle his funnybone.

As well as deadwood, Mother Nature has pruned a few powerlines out by Tarker Brook this wild March night; the sleet has coated the big lines, growing heavier and heavier, until they have parted and fallen on the road like a nest of snakes, lazily turning and spitting blue fire.

All of Tarker's Mills goes dark.

As if finally satisfied, the storm begins to slack off, and not long before midnight the temperature has plummeted from thirty-three degrees to sixteen. Slush freezes solid in weird sculptures. Old Man Hague's hayfield—known locally as Forty

39

Acre Field—takes on a cracked glaze look. The houses remain dark; oil furnaces tick and cool. No linesman is yet able to get up the skating-rink roads.

The clouds pull apart. A full moon slips in and out between the remnants. The ice coating Main Street glows like dead bone.

In the night, something begins to howl.

Later, no one will be able to say where the sound came from; it was everywhere and nowhere as the full moon painted the darkened houses of the village, everywhere and nowhere as the March wind began to rise and moan like a dead Berserker winding his horn, it drifted on the wind, lonely and savage.

Donna Lee hears it as her unpleasant husband sleeps the sleep of the just beside her; constable Neary hears it as he stands at the bedroom window of his Laurel Street apartment in his longhandles; Ollie Parker, the fat and ineffectual grammar school principal hears it in his own bedroom; others hear it, as well. One of them is a boy in a wheelchair.

No one sees it. And no one knows the name of the drifter the linesman found the next morning when he finally got out by Tarker Brook to repair the downed cables. The drifter was coated with ice, head cocked back in a silent scream, ragged old coat and shirt beneath chewed open. The drifter sat in a frozen pool of his own blood, staring at the downed lines, his hands still held up in a warding-off gesture with ice between the fingers.

And all around him are pawprints.

Wolfprints.

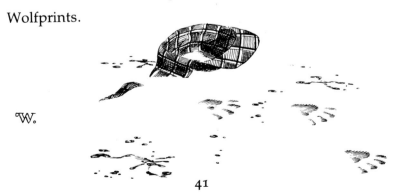

W.

41

JANUARY
FEBRUARY
MARCH
APRIL
MAY
JUNE
JULY
AUGUST
SEPTEMBER
OCTOBER
NOVEMBER
DECEMBER

APRIL

WRIGHTSON 1981

By the middle of the month, the last of the snow flurries have turned to showers of rain and something amazing is happening in Tarker's Mills: it is starting to green up. The ice in Matty Tellingham's cow-pond has gone out, and the patches of snow in the tract of forest called the Big Woods have all begun to shrink. It seems that the old and wonderful trick is going to happen again. Spring is going to come.

The townsfolk celebrate it in small ways in spite of the shadow that has fallen over the town. Gramma Hague bakes pies and sets them out on the kitchen windowsill to cool. On Sunday, at the Grace Baptist Church, the Reverend Lester Lowe reads from The Song of Solomon and preaches a sermon titled "The Spring of the Lord's Love." On a more secular note, Chris Wrightson, the biggest drunk in Tarker's Mills, throws his Great Spring Drunk and staggers off in the silvery, unreal light of a nearly full April moon. Billy Robertson, bartender and proprietor of the pub, Tarker's Mills' only saloon, watches him go and mutters to the barmaid, "If that wolf takes someone tonight, I guess it'll be Chris."

"Don't talk about it," the barmaid replies, shuddering. Her name is Elise Fournier, she is twenty-four, and she attends the Grace Baptist and sings in the choir because she has a crush on the Rev. Lowe. But she plans to leave the Mills by summer; crush or no crush, this wolf business has begun to scare her. She has begun to think that the tips might be better in Portsmouth . . . and the only wolves there wore sailors' uniforms.

Nights in Tarker's Mills as the moon grows fat for the third time that year are uncomfortable times . . . the days are better. On the town common, there is suddenly a skyful of kites each afternoon.

Brady Kincaid, eleven years old, has gotten a Vulture for his birthday and has lost all track of time in his pleasure at feeling the kite tug in his hands like a live thing, watching it dip and swoop through the blue sky above the bandstand. He has forgotten about going home for supper, he is unaware that the other kite-fliers have left one by one, with their box-kites and

47

tent-kites and Aluminum Fliers tucked securely under their arms, unaware that he is alone.

It is the fading daylight and advancing blue shadows which finally make him realize he has lingered too long—that, and the moon just rising over the woods at the edge of the park. For the first time it is a warm-weather moon, bloated and orange instead of a cold white, but Brady doesn't notice this; he is only aware that he has stayed too long, his father is probably going to whup him . . . and dark is coming.

At school, he has laughed at his schoolmates' fanciful tales of the werewolf they say killed the drifter last month, Stella Randolph the month before, Arnie Westrum the month before that. But he doesn't laugh now. As the moon turns April dusk into a bloody furnace-glow, the stories seem all too real.

He begins to wind twine onto his ball as fast as he can, dragging the Vulture with its two bloodshot eyes out of the darkening sky. He brings it in too fast, and the breeze suddenly dies. As a result, the kite dives behind the bandstand.

He starts toward it, winding up string as he goes, glancing nervously back over his shoulder . . . and suddenly the string begins to twitch and move in his hands, sawing back and forth. It reminds him of the way his fishing pole feels when he's hooked a big one in Tarker's Stream, above the Mills. He looks at it, frowning, and the line goes slack.

A shattering roar suddenly fills the night and Brady Kincaid screams. He believes *now*, Yes, he believes *now*, all right, but it's too late and his scream is lost under that snarling roar that rises in a sudden, chilling glissade to a howl.

The wolf is running toward him, running on two legs, its shaggy pelt painted orange with moonfire, its eyes glaring green lamps, and in one paw—a paw with human fingers and claws where the nails should be—is Brady's Vulture kite. It is fluttering madly.

Brady turns to run and dry arms suddenly encircle him; he can smell something like blood and cinnamon, and he is found the next day propped against the War Memorial, headless and disembowelled, the Vulture kite in one stiffening hand.

The kite flutters, as if trying for the sky, as the search-party turn away, horrified and sick. It flutters because the breeze has already come up. It flutters as if it knows this will be a good day for kites.

JANUARY
FEBRUARY
MARCH
APRIL
MAY
JUNE
JULY
AUGUST
SEPTEMBER
OCTOBER
NOVEMBER
DECEMBER

MAY

WRIGHTSON
1983

On the night before Homecoming Sunday at the Grace Baptist Church, the Reverend Lester Lowe has a terrible dream from which he awakes, trembling, bathed in sweat, staring at the narrow windows of the parsonage. Through them, across the road, he can see his church. Moonlight falls through the parsonage's bedroom windows in still silver beams, and for one moment he fully expects to see the werewolf the old codgers have all been whispering about. Then he closes his eyes, begging for forgiveness for his superstitious lapse, finishing his prayer by whispering the "For Jesus' sake, amen"—so his mother taught him to end all his prayers.

Ah, but the dream...

In his dream it was tomorrow and he had been preaching the Homecoming Sermon. The church is always filled on Homecoming Sunday (only the oldest of the old codgers still call it Old Home Sunday now), and instead of looking out on pews half or wholly empty as he does on most Sundays, every bench is full.

In his dream he has been preaching with a fire and a force that he rarely attains in reality (he tends to drone, which may be one reason that Grace Baptist's attendance has fallen off so drastically in the last ten years or so). This morning his tongue seems to have been touched with the Pentecostal Fire, and he realizes that he is preaching the greatest sermon of his life, and its subject is this: THE BEAST WALKS AMONG US. Over and over he hammers at the point, vaguely aware that his voice has grown roughly strong, that his words have attained an almost poetic rhythm.

The Beast, he tells them, is everywhere. The Great Satan, he tells them, can be anywhere. At a high school dance. Buying a deck of Marlboros and a Bic butane lighter down at the Trading Post. Standing in front of Brighton's Drug, eating a Slim Jim, and waiting for the 4:40 Greyhound from Bangor to pull in. The Beast might be sitting next to you at a band concert or having a piece of pie at the Chat 'n Chew on Main Street. The Beast, he tells them, his voice dropping to a whisper that throbs, and no eye wanders. He has them in thrall. Watch for the Beast, for he may smile and say he is your neighbor, but oh my brethren, his teeth are sharp and you may mark the uneasy way in which his eyes roll. He is the Beast, and he is here, now, in Tarker's Mills. He—

But here he breaks off, his eloquence gone, because something terrible is happening out there in his sunny church. His congregation is beginning to change, and he realizes with horror that they are turning into werewolves, all of them, all three hundred of them: Victor Bowle, the head selectman, usually so white and fat and pudgy . . . his skin is turning brown, roughening, darkening with hair! Violet MacKenzie, who teaches piano . . . her narrow spinster's body is filling out, her thin nose flattening and splaying! The fat science teacher, Elbert Freeman, seems to be growing fatter, his shiny blue suit is splitting, clocksprings of hair are bursting out like the stuffing from an old sofa! His fat lips split back like bladders to reveal teeth the size of piano keys!

The Beast, the Rev. Lowe tries to say in his dreams, but the words fail him and he stumbles back from the pulpit in horror as Cal Blodwin, the Grace Baptist's head deacon, shambles down the center aisle, snarling, money spilling from the silver collection plate, his head cocked to one side. Violet MacKenzie leaps on him and they roll in the aisle together, biting and shrieking in voices which are almost human.

And now the others join in and the sound is like the zoo at feeding-time, and this time the Rev. Lowe *screams* it out, in a kind of ecstasy: *"The Beast! The Beast is everywhere! Everywhere! Every—"* But his voice is no longer his voice; it has become an inarticulate snarling sound, and when he looks down, he sees the hands protruding from the sleeves of his good black suitcoat have become snaggled paws.

And then he awakes.

Only a dream, he thinks, lying back down again. *Only a dream, thank God.*

But when he opens the church doors that morning, the morning of Homecoming Sunday, the morning after the full moon, it is no dream he sees; it is the gutted body of Clyde Corliss, who has done janitorial work for years, hanging face-down over the pulpet. His push-broom leans close by.

None of this is a dream; the Rev. Lowe only wishes it could be. He opens his mouth, hitches in a great, gasping breath, and begins to scream.

Spring has come back again—and this year, the Beast has come with it.

JANUARY
FEBRUARY
MARCH
APRIL
MAY
JUNE
JULY
AUGUST
SEPTEMBER
OCTOBER
NOVEMBER
DECEMBER

On the shortest night of the year, Alfie Knopfler, who runs the Chat 'n Chew, Tarker's Mills' only cafe, polishes his long Formica counter to a gleaming brightness, the sleeves of his white shirt rolled to past his muscular, tattooed elbows. The cafe is for the moment completely empty, and as he finishes with the counter, he pauses for a moment, looking out into the street, thinking that he lost his virginity on a fragrant early summer night like this one—the girl had been Arlene McCune, who is now Arlene Bessey, and married to one of Bangor's most successful young lawyers. God, how she had moved that night on the back seat of his car, and how sweet the night had smelled!

The door into summer swings open and lets in a bright tide of moonlight. He supposes the cafe is deserted because the Beast is supposed to walk when the moon in full, but Alfie is neither scared nor worried; not scared because he weighs two-twenty and most of it is still good old Navy muscle, not worried because he knows the regulars will be in bright and early to-morrow morning for their eggs and their homefries and coffee. Maybe, he thinks, I'll close her up a little early tonight—shut off the coffee urn, button her up, get a six-pack down at the Market Basket, and take in the second picture at the drive-in. June, June, full moon—a good night for the drive-in and a few beers. A good night to remember the conquests of the past.

He is turning toward the coffee-maker when the door opens, and he turns back, resigned.

"Say! How you doin'?" he asks, because the customer is one of his regulars . . . although he rarely sees this customer later than ten in the morning.

The customer nods, and the two of them pass a few friendly words.

"Coffee?" Alfie asks, as the customer slips onto one of the padded red counter-stools.

"Please."

Well, still time to catch that second show, Alfie thinks, turning to the coffee-maker. He don't look like he's good for long. Tired. Sick, maybe. Still plenty of time to—

Shock wipes out the rest of his thought. Alfie gapes stupidly. The coffee-maker is as spotless as everything else in the Chat 'n Chew, the stainless steel cylinder bright as a metal mirror. And in its smoothly bulging convex surface he sees something as unbelievable as it is hideous. His customer, someone he sees every day, someone *everyone* in Tarker's Mills sees every day, is changing. The customer's face is somehow shifting, melting, thickening, broadening. The customer's cotton shirt is stretching, stretching... and suddenly the shirt's seams begin to pull apart, and absurdly, all Alfie Knopfler can think of is that show his little nephew Ray used to like to watch, *The Incredible Hulk*.

The customer's pleasant, unremarkable face is becoming something bestial. The customer's mild brown eyes have lightened; have become a terrible gold-green. The customer screams ... but the scream breaks apart, drops like an elevator through registers of sound, and becomes a bellowing growl of rage.

It—the thing, the Beast, werewolf, whatever it is—gropes at the smooth Formica and knocks over a sugar-shaker. It grabs the thick glass cylinder as it rolls, spraying sugar, and heaves it at the wall where the specials are taped up, still bellowing.

Alfie wheels around and his hip knocks the coffee urn off the shelf. It hits the floor with a bang and sprays hot coffee everywhere, burning his ankles. He cries out in pain and fear. Yes, he is afraid now, his two hundred and twenty pounds of good Navy muscle are forgotten now, his nephew Ray is forgotten now, his back seat coupling with Arlene McCune is forgotten now, and there is only the Beast, here now like some horror-monster in a drive-in movie, a horror-monster that has come right out of the screen.

It leaps on top of the counter with a terrible muscular ease, its slacks in tatters, its shirt in rags. Alfie can hear keys and change jingling in its pockets.

It leaps at Alfie, and Alfie tries to dodge, but he trips over the coffee urn and goes sprawling on the red linoleum. There is another shattering roar, a flood of warm yellow breath, and then a great red pain as the creature's jaws sink into the deltoid muscles of his back and rip upward with terrifying force. Blood sprays the floor, the counter, the grille.

Alfie staggers to his feet with a huge, ragged, spraying hole in his back; he is trying to scream, and white moonlight, summer moonlight, floods in through the windows and dazzles his eyes.

The Beast leaps on him again.

Moonlight is the last thing Alfie sees.

JANUARY
FEBRUARY
MARCH
APRIL
MAY
JUNE
JULY
AUGUST
SEPTEMBER
OCTOBER
NOVEMBER
DECEMBER

They cancelled the Fourth of July.

Marty Coslaw gets remarkably little sympathy from the people closest to him when he tells them that. Perhaps it is because they simply don't understand the depth of his pain.

"Don't be foolish," his mother tells him brusquely—she is often brusque with him, and when she has to rationalize this brusqueness to herself, she tells herself she will not spoil the boy just because he is handicapped, because he is going to spend his life sitting in a wheelchair.

"Wait until next year!" his dad tells him, clapping him on the back. "Twice as good! Twice as doodly-damn good! You'll see, little bitty buddy! Hey, hey!"

Herman Coslaw is the phys ed teacher at the Tarker's Mills grammar school, and he almost always talks to his son in what Marty thinks of as dad's Big Pal voice. He also says "Hey, hey!" a great deal. The truth is, Marty makes Herman Coslaw a little nervous. Herman lives in a world of violently active children, kids who run races, bash baseballs, swim rally sprints. And in the midst of directing all this he would sometimes look up and see Marty, somewhere close by, sitting in his wheelchair, watching. It made Herman nervous, and when he was nervous, he spoke in his bellowing Big Pal voice, and said "Hey, hey!" or "doodly-damn" and called Marty his "little bitty buddy."

"Ha-ha, so you finally didn't get something you wanted!" his big sister says when he tries to tell her how he had looked forward to this night, how he looks forward to it every year, the flowers of light in the sky over the Commons, the flashgun pops of brightness followed by the thudding *KER-WHAMP!* sounds that roll back and forth between the low hills that surrounded the town. Kate is thirteen to Marty's ten, and convinced that everyone loves Marty just because he can't walk. She is delighted that the fireworks have been cancelled.

Even Grandfather Coslaw, who could usually be counted on for sympathy, hadn't been impressed. "Nobody is cancellin der fort of Choo-lie, boy," he said in his heavy Slavic accent. He was sitting on the verandah, and Marty buzzed out through the french doors in his battery-powered wheelchair to talk to him. Grandfather Coslaw sat looking down the slope of the lawn toward the woods, a glass of schnapps in one hand. This had happened on July 2, two days ago. "It's just the fireworks they cancel. And you know why."

Marty did. The killer, that was why. In the papers now they were calling him The Full Moon Killer, but Marty had heard plenty of whispers around school before classes had ended for the summer. Lots of kids were saying that The Full Moon Killer wasn't a real man at all, but some sort of supernatural creature. A werewolf, maybe. Marty didn't believe that—werewolves were strictly for the horror movies—but he supposed there could be some kind of crazy guy out there who only felt the urge to kill when the moon was full. The fireworks have been cancelled because of their dirty rotten *curfew*.

In January, sitting in his wheelchair by the french doors and looking out onto the verandah, watching the wind blow bitter veils of snow across the frozen crust, or standing by the front door, stiff as a statue in his locked leg-braces, watching the other kids pull their sleds toward Wright's Hill, just *thinking* of the fireworks made a difference. Thinking of a warm summer night, a cold Coke, of fire-roses blooming in the dark, and pinwheels, and an American flag made of Roman candles.

But now they have cancelled the fireworks . . . and no matter what anyone says, Marty feels that it is really the Fourth *itself—his* Fourth—that they have done to death.

Only his Uncle Al, who blew into town late this morning to have the traditional salmon and fresh peas with the family, had understood. He had listened closely, standing on the verandah tiles in his dripping bathing suit (the others were swimming and laughing in the Coslaws' new pool on the other side of the house) after lunch.

Marty finished and looked at Uncle Al anxiously.

"Do you see what I mean? Do you get it? It hasn't got anything to do with being crippled, like Katie says, or getting the fireworks all mixed up with America, like Granpa thinks. It's just not right, when you look forward to something for so long ... it's not right for Victor Bowle and some dumb town *council* to come along and take it away. Not when it's something you really need. Do you get it?"

There was a long, agonizing pause while Uncle Al considered Marty's question. Time enough for Marty to hear the kick-rattle of the diving board at the deep end of the pool, followed by Dad's hearty bellow: "Lookin' good, Kate! Hey, hey! Lookin' *reeeeeel ... good!*"

Then Uncle Al said quietly: "Sure I get it. And I got something for you, I think. Maybe you can make your own Fourth."

"My own Fourth? What do you mean?"

"Come on out to my car, Marty. I've got something ... well, I'll show you." And he was striding away along the concrete path that circled the house before Marty could ask him what he meant.

His wheelchair hummed along the path to the driveway, away from the sounds of the pool—splashes, laughing screams, the *kathummmm* of the diving board. Away from his father's booming Big Pal voice. The sound of his wheelchair was a low, steady hum that Marty barely heard—all his life that sound, and the clank of his braces, had been the music of his movement.

Uncle Al's car was a low-slung Mercedes convertible. Marty knew his parents disapproved of it ("Twenty-eight-thousand-dollar deathtrap," his mother had once called it with a brusque little sniff), but Marty loved it. Once Uncle Al had taken him for a ride on some of the back roads that crisscrossed Tarker's Mills, and he had driven fast—seventy, maybe eighty. He wouldn't tell Marty how fast they were going. "If you don't know, you won't be scared," he had said. But Marty hadn't been scared. His belly had been sore the next day from laughing.

Uncle Al took something out of the glove-compartment of his car, and as Marty rolled up and stopped, he put a bulky cellophane package on the boy's withered thighs. "Here you go, kid," he said. "Happy Fourth of July."

The first thing Marty saw were exotic Chinese markings on the package's label. Then he saw what was inside, and his heart seemed to squeeze up in his chest. The cellophane package was full of fireworks.

"The ones that look like pyramids are Twizzers," Uncle Al said.

Marty, absolutely stunned with joy, moved his lips to speak, but nothing came out.

"Light the fuses, set them down, and they spray as many colors as there are on a dragon's breath. The tubes with the thin sticks coming out of them are bottle-rockets. Put them in an empty Coke bottle and up they go. The little ones are fountains. There are two Roman candles . . . and of course, a package of firecrackers. But you better set those off tomorrow."

Uncle Al cast an eye toward the noises coming from the pool.

"Thank you!" Marty was finally able to gasp. "Thank you, Uncle Al!"

"Just keep mum about where you got them," Uncle Al said. "A nod's as good as a wink to a blind horse, right?"

"Right, right," Marty babbled, although he had no idea what nods, winks, and blind horses had to do with fireworks. "But are you sure you don't want them, Uncle Al?"

"I can get more," Uncle Al said. "I know a guy over in Bridgton. He'll be doing business until it gets dark." He put a hand on Marty's head. "You keep your Fourth after everyone else goes to bed. Don't shoot off any of the noisy ones and wake them all up. And for Christ's sake don't blow your hand off, or my big sis will never speak to me again."

Then Uncle Al laughed and climbed into his car and roared the engine into life. He raised his hand in a half-salute to Marty and then was gone while Marty was still trying to stutter his thanks. He sat there for a moment looking after his uncle, swallowing hard to keep from crying. Then he put the packet of fireworks into his shirt and buzzed back to the house and his room. In his mind he was already waiting for night to come and everyone to be asleep.

He is the first one in bed that night. His mother comes in and kisses him goodnight (brusquely, not looking at his stick-like legs under the sheet). "You okay, Marty?"

"Yes, mom."

She pauses, as if to say something more, and then gives her head a little shake. She leaves.

His sister Kate comes in. She doesn't kiss him; merely leans her head close to his neck so he can smell the chlorine in her hair and she whispers: "See? you don't always get what you want just because you're a cripple."

"You might be surprised what I get," he says softly, and she regards him for a moment with narrow suspicion before going out.

His father comes in last and sits on the side of Marty's bed. He speaks in his booming Big Pal voice. "Everything okay, big guy? You're off to bed early. *Real* early."

"Just feeling a little tired, daddy."

"Okay." He slaps one of Marty's wasted legs with his big hand, winces unconsciously, and then gets up in a hurry. "Sorry about the fireworks, but just wait till next year! Hey, hey! Rootie-patootie!"

Marty smiles a small, secret smile.

75

So then he begins the waiting for the rest of the house to go to bed. It takes a long time. The TV runs on and on in the living room, the canned laughtracks often augmented by Katie's shrill giggles. The toilet in Granpa's bedroom goes with a bang and a flush. His mother chats on the phone, wishes someone a happy Fourth, says yes, it was a shame the fireworks show had been cancelled, but she thought that, under the circumstances, everyone understood why it had to be. Yes, Marty had been disappointed. Once, near the end of her conversation, she laughs, and when she laughs, she doesn't sound a bit brusque. She hardly ever laughs around Marty.

Every now and then, as seven-thirty became eight and nine, his hand creeps under his pillow to make sure the cellophane bag of fireworks is still there. Around nine-thirty, when the moon gets high enough to peer into his window and flood his room with silvery light, the house finally begins to wind down.

The TV clicks off. Katie goes to bed, protesting that all her friends got to stay up *late* in the summer. After she's gone, Marty's folks sit in the parlor awhile longer, their conversation only murmurs. And . . .

. . . and maybe he slept, because when he next touches the wonderful bag of fireworks, he realizes that the house is totally still and the moon has become even brighter—bright enough to cast shadows. He takes the bag out along with the book of matches he found earlier. He tucks his pajama shirt into his pajama pants; drops both the bag and the matches into his shirt, and prepares to get out of bed.

This is an operation for Marty, but not a painful one, as people sometimes seemed to think. There is no feeling of any kind in his legs, so there can be no pain. He grips the headboard of the bed, pulls himself up to a sitting position, and then shifts his legs over the edge of the bed one by one. He does this one-handed, using his other hand to hold the rail which begins at his bed and runs all the way around the room. Once he had tried moving his legs with both hands and somersaulted help-

lessly head over heels onto the floor. The crash brought everyone running. "You stupid show-off!" Kate had whispered
fiercely into his ear after he had been helped into his chair, a
little shaken up but laughing crazily in spite of the swelling on
one temple and his split lip. "You want to kill yourself? Huh?"
And then she had run out of the room, crying.

Once he's sitting on the edge of the bed, he wipes his hands
on the front of his shirt to make sure they're dry and won't
slip. Then he uses the rail to go hand over hand to his wheelchair. His useless scarecrow legs, so much dead weight, drag
along behind him. The moonlight is bright enough to cast his
shadow, bright and crisp, on the floor ahead of him.

His wheelchair is on the brake, and he swings into it with
confident ease. He pauses for a moment, catching his breath,
listening to the silence of the house. *Don't shoot off any of the
noisy ones tonight,* Uncle Al had said, and listening to the silence,
Marty knows that was right. He will keep his Fourth by himself
and to himself and no one will know. At least not until tomorrow when they see the blackened husks of the twizzers
and the fountains out on the verandah, and then it wouldn't
matter. *As many colors as there are on a dragon's breath,* Uncle Al
had said. But Marty supposes there's no law against a dragon
breathing silently.

He lets the brake off his chair and flips the power switch.
The little amber eye, the one that means his battery is well-
charged, comes on in the dark. Marty pushes RIGHT TURN.
The chair rotates right. Hey, hey. When it is facing the verandah
doors, he pushes FORWARD. The chair rolls forward, hum-
ming quietly.

Marty slips the latch on the double doors, pushes FORWARD
again, and rolls outside. He tears open the wonderful bag of
fireworks and then pauses for a moment, captivated by the
summer night—the somnolent chirr of the crickets, the low,
fragrant breeze that barely stirs the leaves of the trees at the
edge of the woods, the almost unearthly radiance of the moon.

He can wait no longer. He brings out a snake, strikes a match, lights its fuse, and watches in entranced silence as it splutters green-blue fire and grows magically, writhing and spitting flame from its tail.

The Fourth, he thinks, his eyes alight. *The Fourth, the Fourth, happy Fourth of July to me!*

The snake's bright flame gutters low, flickers, goes out. Marty lights one of the triangular twizzers and watches as it spouts fire as yellow as his dad's lucky golf shirt. Before it can go out, he lights a second that shoots off light as dusky-red as the roses which grow beside the picket fence around the new pool. Now a wonderful smell of spent powder fills the night for the wind to rafter and pull slowly away.

His groping hands pull out the flat packet of firecrackers next, and he has opened them before he realizes that to light these would be calamity—their jumping, snapping, machine-gun roar would wake the whole neighborhood: fire, flood, alarm, excursion. All of those, and one ten-year-old boy named Martin Coslaw in the doghouse until Christmas, most likely.

He pushes the Black Cats further up on his lap, gropes happily in the bag again, and comes out with the biggest twizzer of all—a World Class Twizzer if ever there was one. It is almost as big as his closed fist. He lights it with mixed fright and delight, and tosses it.

Red light as bright as hellfire fills the night...and it is by this shifting, feverish glow that Marty sees the bushes at the fringe of the woods below the verandah shake and part. There is a low noise, half-cough, half-snarl. The Beast appears.

It stands for a moment at the base of the lawn and seems to scent the air...and then it begins to shamble up the slope toward where Marty sits on the slate flagstones in his wheelchair, his eyes bulging, his upper body shrinking against the canvas back of his chair. The Beast is hunched over, but it is clearly walking on its two rear legs. Walking the way a man would walk. The red light of the twizzer skates hellishly across its green eyes.

It moves slowly, its wide nostrils flaring rhythmically. Scenting prey, almost surely scenting that prey's weakness. Marty can *smell* it—its hair, its sweat, its savagery. It grunts again. Its thick upper lip, the color of liver, wrinkles back to show its heavy tusk-like teeth. Its pelt is painted a dull silvery-red.

It has almost reached him—its clawed hands, so like-unlike human hands, reaching for his throat—when the boy remembers the packet of firecrackers. Hardly aware he is going to do it, he strikes a match and touches it to the master fuse. The fuse spits a hot line of red sparks that singe the fine hair on the back of his hand, crisping them. The werewolf, momentarily offbalance, draws backwards, uttering a questioning grunt that, like his hands, is nearly human. Marty throws the packet of firecrackers in its face.

They go off in a banging, flashing train of light and sound. The beast utters a screech-roar of pain and rage; it staggers backwards, clawing at the explosions that tattoo grains of fire and burning gunpowder into its face. Marty sees one of its lamplike green eyes whiff out as four crackers go off at once with a terrific thundering KA-POW! at the side of its muzzle. Now its screams are pure agony. It claws at its face, bellowing, and as the first lights go on in the Coslaw house it turns and bounds back down the lawn toward the woods, leaving behind it only a smell of singed fur and the first frightened and bewildered cries from the house.

"What was that?" His mother's voice, not sounding a bit brusque.

"Who's there, goddammit?" His father, not sounding very much like a Big Pal.

"Marty?" Kate, her voice quavering, not sounding mean at all. "Marty, are you all right?"

Grandfather Coslaw sleeps through the whole thing.

Marty leans back in his wheelchair as the big red twizzer gutters its way to extinction. Its light is now the mild and lovely pink of an early sunrise. He is too shocked to weep. But his shock is not entirely a dark emotion, although the next day his parents will bundle him off to visit his Uncle Jim and Aunt Ida over in Stowe, Vermont, where he will stay until the end of summer vacation (the police concur; they feel that The Full Moon Killer might try to attack Marty again, and silence him). There is a deep exultation in him. It is stronger than the shock. He has looked into the terrible face of the Beast and lived. And there is simple, childlike joy in him, as well, a quiet joy he will never be able to communicate later to anyone, not even Uncle Al, who might have understood. He feels this joy because the fireworks have happened after all.

And while his parents stewed and wondered about his psyche, and if he would have complexes from the experience, Marty Coslaw came to believe in his heart that it had been the best Fourth of all.

JANUARY
FEBRUARY
MARCH
APRIL
MAY
JUNE
JULY
AUGUST
SEPTEMBER
OCTOBER
NOVEMBER
DECEMBER

AUGUST

WRIGHTSON 1983

"Sure, I think it's a werewolf," Constable Neary says. He speaks too loudly—maybe accidentally, more like accidentally on purpose—and all conversation in Stan's Barber Shop comes to a halt. It is going on just half-past August, the hottest August anyone can remember in Tarker's Mills for years, and tonight the moon will be just one day past full. So the town holds its breath, waiting.

Constable Neary surveys his audience and then goes on from his place in Stan Pelky's middle barber chair, speaking weightily, speaking judicially, speaking psychologically, all from the depths of his high school education (Neary is a big, beefy man, and in high school he mostly made touchdowns for the Tarker's Mills Tigers; his classwork earned him some C's and not a few D's).

"There are guys," he tells them, "who are kind of like two people. Kind of like split personalities, you know. They are what I'd call fucking schizos."

He pauses to appreciate the respectful silence which greets this and then goes on:

"Now this guy, I think he's like that. I don't think he knows what he's doing when the moon gets full and he goes out and kills somebody. He could be anybody—a teller at the bank, a gas-jockey at one of those stations out on the Town Road, maybe even someone right here now. In the sense of being an animal inside and looking perfectly normal outside, yeah, you bet. But if you mean, do I think there's a guy who sprouts hair and howls at the moon . . . no. That shit's for kids."

"What about the Coslaw boy, Neary?" Stan asks, continuing to work carefully around the roll of fat at the base of Neary's neck. His long, sharp scissors go *snip . . . snip . . . snip.*

"Just proves what I said," Neary responds with some exasperation. "That shit's for kids."

In truth, he *feels* exasperated about what's happened with Marty Coslaw. Here, in this boy, is the first eyeball witness to the freak that's killed six people in his town, including Neary's good friend Alfie Knopfler. And is he allowed to interview the boy? No. Does he even know where the boy is? No! He's had to make do with a deposition furnished to him by the State Police, and he had to bow and scrape and just-a-damn-bout *beg* to get that much. All because he's a small-town constable, what the State Police think of as a kiddie-cop, not able to tie his own shoes. All because he doesn't have one of their numbfuck Smokey Bear hats. And the deposition! He might as well have used it to wipe his ass with. According to the Coslaw kid, this "beast" stood about seven feet tall, was naked, was covered with dark hair all over his body. He had big teeth and green eyes and smelled like a load of panther-shit. He had claws, but the claws looked like hands. He thought it had a tail. *A tail,* for Chrissake.

"Maybe," Kenny Franklin says from his place in the row of chairs along the wall, "maybe it's some kind of disguise this fella puts on. Like a mask and all, you know."

"I don't believe it," Neary says emphatically, and nods his head to emphasize the point. Stan has to draw his scissors back in a hurry to avoid putting one of the blades into that beefy roll of fat at the back of Neary's neck. "Nossir! I don't believe it! Kid heard a lot of these werewolf stories at school before it closed for the summer—he admitted as much—and then he didn't have nothing to do but sit there in that chair of his and think about it . . . work it over in his mind. It's all psycho-fuckin-logical, you see. Why, if it'd been *you* that'd come out of the bushes by the light of the moon, he would have thought *you* was a wolf, Kenny."

Kenny laughs a little uneasily.

"Nope," Neary says gloomily. "Kid's testimony is just no damn good 'tall."

In his disgust and disappointment over the deposition taken from Marty Coslaw at the home of Marty's aunt and uncle in Stowe, Constable Neary has also overlooked this line: "Four of

them went off at the side of his face—I guess you'd call it a face—all at once, and I guess maybe it put his eye out. His left eye."

If Constable Neary had chewed this over in his mind—and he hadn't—he would have laughed even more contemptuously, because in that hot, still August of 1984, there was only one townsperson sporting an eyepatch, and it was simply impossible to think of *that* person, of all persons, being the killer. Neary would have believed his mother the killer before he would have believed *that*.

"There's only one thing that'll solve this case," Constable Neary says, jabbing his finger at the four or five men sitting against the wall and waiting for their Saturday morning haircuts, "and that's good police work. And I intend to be the guy who does it. Those state Smokies are going to be laughing on the other side of their faces when I bring the guy in." Neary's face turns dreamy. "Anyone," he says. "A bank teller . . . gas jockey . . . just some guy you drink with down there at the bar. But good police-work will solve it. You mark my words."

But Constable Lander Neary's good police work comes to an end that night when a hairy, moon-silvered arm reaches through the open window of his Dodge pickup as he sits parked at the crossing-point of two dirt roads out in West Tarker's Mills. There is a low, snorting grunt, and a wild, terrifying smell— like something you would smell in the lion-house of a zoo.

His head is snapped around and he stares into one green eye. He sees the fur, the black, damp-looking snout. And when the snout wrinkles back, he sees the teeth. The beast claws at him almost playfully, and one of his cheeks is ripped away in a flap, exposing his teeth on the right side. Blood spouts everywhere. He can feel it running down over the shoulder of his shirt, sinking in warmly. He screams; he screams out of his mouth and out of his cheek. Over the beast's working shoulders, he can see the moon, flooding down white light.

He forgets all about his .30-.30 and the .45 strapped on

his belt. He forgets all about how this thing is psycho-fuckin-logical. He forgets all about good police work. Instead his mind fixes on something Kenny Franklin said in the barber-shop that morning. *Maybe it's some kind of disguise this fella puts on. Like a mask and all, you know.*

And so, as the werewolf reaches for Neary's throat, Neary reaches for its face, grabs double-handfuls of coarse, wiry fur and pulls, hoping madly that the mask will shift and then pull off—there will be the snap of an elastic, the liquid ripping sound of latex, and he will see the killer.

But nothing happens—nothing except a roar of pain and rage from the beast. It swipes at him with one clawed hand—yes, he can see it is a hand, however hideously misshapen, a *hand*, the boy was right—and lays his throat wide open. Blood jets over the truck's windshield and dashboard; it drips into the bottle of Busch that has been sitting tilted against Constable Neary's crotch.

The werewolf's other hand snags in Neary's freshly cut hair and yanks him half out of the Ford pick-up's cab. It howls once, in triumph, and then it buries its face and snout in Neary's neck. It feeds while the beer gurgles out of the spilled bottle and foams on the floor by the truck's brake and clutch pedals.

So much for psychology.

So much for good police work.

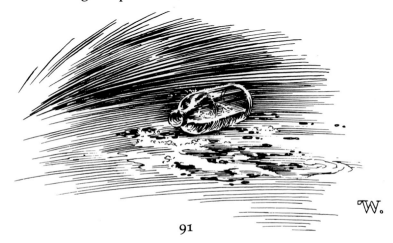

JANUARY
FEBRUARY
MARCH
APRIL
MAY
JUNE
JULY
AUGUST
SEPTEMBER
OCTOBER
NOVEMBER
DECEMBER

WRIGHTSON 1983

As the month wears on and the night of the full moon approaches again, the frightened people of Tarker's Mills wait for a break in the heat, but no such break comes. Elsewhere, in the wider world, the baseball divisional races are decided one by one and the football exhibition season has begun; in the Canadian Rockies, jolly old Willard Scott informs the people of Tarker's Mills, a foot of snow falls on the twenty-first of September. But in this corner of the world summer hangs right in there. Temperatures linger in the eighties during the days; kids, three weeks back in school and not happy to be there sit and swelter in droning classrooms where the clocks seem to have been set to click only one minute forward for each hour which passes in real time. Husbands and wives argue viciously for no reason, and at O'Neil's Gulf Station out on Town Road by the entrance to the turnpike, a tourist starts giving Pucky O'Neil some lip about the price of gas and Pucky brains the fellow with the gas-pump nozzle. The fellow, who is from New Jersey, needs four stitches in his upper lip and goes away muttering balefully under his breath about lawsuits and subpeonas.

"I don't know what he's bitching about," Pucky says sullenly that night in the Pub. "I only hit him with half of my force, you know? If I'd'a hit him with *all* my force, I woulda knocked his frockin smart mouth right the frock off. You know?"

"Sure," Billy Robertson says, because Pucky looks like he may hit *him* with all his force if he disagrees. "How about another beer, Puck?"

"Your frockin-A," Pucky says.

Milt Sturmfuller puts his wife in the hospital over a bit of egg that the dishwasher didn't take off one of the plates. He takes one look at that dried yellow smear on the plate she tried to give him for his lunch, and pounds her a good one. As Pucky O'Neil would have said, Milt hits her with all his force. "Damn slutty bitch," he says, standing over Donna Lee, who is sprawled out on the kitchen floor, her nose broken and bleeding, the back of her head also bleeding. "My mother used to get the

97

dishes clean, and she didn't have no dishwasher, either. What's the matter with *you?*" Later, Milt will tell the doctor at the Portland General Hospital emergency room that Donna Lee fell down the back stairs. Donna Lee, terrorized and cowed after nine years in a marital war-zone, will back this up.

Around seven o'clock on the night of the full moon, a wind springs up—the first chill wind of that long summer season. It brings a rack of clouds from the north and for awhile the moon plays tag with these clouds, ducking in and out of them, turning their edges to beaten silver. Then the clouds grow thicker, and the moon disappears ... yet it is there; the tides twenty miles out of Tarker's Mills feel its pull and so, closer to home, does the Beast.

Around two in the morning, a dreadful squealing arises from the pigpen of Elmer Zinneman on the West Stage Road, about twelve miles out of town. Elmer goes for his rifle, wearing only his pajama pants and his slippers. His wife, who was almost pretty when Elmer married her at sixteen in 1947, pleads and begs and cries, wanting him to stay with her, wanting him not to go out. Elmer shakes her off and grabs his gun from the entryway. His pigs are not just squealing; they are *screaming.* They sound like a bunch of very young girls surprised by a maniac at a slumber party. He is going, nothing can make him not go, he tells her ... and then freezes with one work-callused hand on the latch of the back door as a screaming howl of triumph rises in the night. It is a wolf-cry, but there is something so human in the howl that it makes his hand drop from the latch and he allows Alice Zinneman to pull him back into the living room. He puts his arms around her and draws her down onto the sofa, and there they sit like two frightened children.

Now the crying of the pigs begins to falter and stop. Yes, they stop. One by one, they stop. Their squeals die in hoarse, bloody gargling sounds. The Beast howls again, its cry as silver as the moon. Elmer goes to the window and sees something— he cannot tell what—go bounding off into the deeper darkness.

The rain comes later, pelting against the windows as Elmer

and Alice sit up in bed together, all the lights in the bedroom on. It is a cold rain, the first real rain of the autumn, and tomorrow the first tinge of color will have come into the leaves.

Elmer finds what he expects in his pig-pen; carnage. All nine of his sows and both of his boars are dead—disembowelled and partly eaten. They lie in the mud, the cold rain pelting down on their carcasses, their bulging eyes staring up at the cold autumn sky.

Elmer's brother Pete, called over from Minot, stands beside Elmer. They don't speak for a long time, and then Elmer says what has been in Pete's mind as well. "Insurance will cover some of it. Not all, but some. I guess I can foot the rest. Better my pigs than another person."

Pete nods. "There's been enough," he says, his voice a murmur that can barely be heard over the rain.

"What do you mean?"

"You know what I mean. Next full moon there's got to be forty men out . . . or sixty . . . or a hundred and sixty. Time folks stopped dicking around and pretending it ain't happening, when any fool can see it is. Look here, for Christ's sweet sake!"

Pete points down. Around the slaughtered pigs, the soft earth of the pen is full of very large tracks. They look like the tracks of a wolf . . . but they also look weirdly human.

"You see those fucking tracks?"

"I see them," Elmer allows.

"You think Sweet Betsy from Pike made those tracks?"

"No. I guess not."

"Werewolf made those tracks," Pete says, "You know it, Alice knows it, most of the people in this town know it. Hell, even *I* know it, and I come from the next county over." He looks at his brother, his face dour and stern, the face of a New

England Puritan from 1650. And he repeats: "There's been enough. Time this thing was ended."

Elmer considers this long as the rain continues to tap on the two men's slickers, and then he nods. "I guess. But not next full moon."

"You want to wait until November?"

Elmer nods. "Bare woods. Better tracking, if we get a little snow."

"What about next month?"

Elmer Zinneman looks at his slaughtered pigs in the pen beside his barn. Then he looks at his brother Pete.

"People better look out," he says.

JANUARY
FEBRUARY
MARCH
APRIL
MAY
JUNE
JULY
AUGUST
SEPTEMBER
OCTOBER
NOVEMBER
DECEMBER

OCTOBER

WRIGHTSON 1983

When Marty Coslaw comes home from trick or treating on Halloween Night with the batteries in his wheelchair all but dead flat, he goes directly to bed, where he lies awake until the half-moon rises in a cold sky strewn with stars like diamond chips. Outside, on the verandah where his life was saved by a string of Fourth of July firecrackers, a chill wind blows brown leaves in swirling, aimless corkscrews on the flagstones. They rattle like old bones. The October full moon has come and gone in Tarker's Mills with no new murder, the second month in a row this has happened. Some of the townspeople—Stan Pelky, the barber, is one, and Cal Blodwin, who owns Blodwin Chevrolet, the town's only car dealership, is another—believe that the terror is over; the killer was a drifter, or a tramp living out in the woods, and now he has moved on, just as they said he would. Others, however, are not so sure. These are the ones who do long reckoning on the four deer found slaughtered out by the turnpike the day after the October full moon, and upon Elmer Zinneman's eleven pigs, killed at full moon time in September. The argument rages at The Pub over beers during the long autumn nights.

But Marty Coslaw knows.

This night he has gone out trick or treating with his father (his father likes Halloween, likes the brisk cold, likes to laugh his hearty Big Pal laugh and bellow such idiotic things as "Hey, hey!" and "Ring-dang-doo!" when the doors open and familiar Tarker's Mills faces look out). Marty went as Yoda, a big rubber Don Post mask pulled down over his head and a voluminous robe on which covered his wasted legs. "You *always* get everything you want," Katie says with a toss of her head when she sees the mask . . . but he knows she isn't really mad at him (and as if to prove it, she makes him an artfully crooked Yoda staff to complete his getup), but perhaps sad because she is now considered too old to go out trick or treating. Instead she will go to a party with her junior high school friends. She will dance to Donna Summer records, and bob for apples, and later on the lights will be turned down for a game of spin-the-bottle and she will perhaps kiss some boy, not because she wants to but because it will be fun to giggle about it with her girlfriends in study hall the next day.

Marty's dad takes Marty in the van because the van has a built-in ramp he can use to get Marty in and out. Marty rolls down the ramp and then buzzes up and down the streets themselves in his chair. He carries his bag on his lap and they go to all the houses on their road and then to a few houses downtown: the Collinses, the MacInnes', the Manchesters', the Millikens', the Eastons'. There is a fishbowl full of candy corn inside The Pub. Snickers Bars at the Congregational Church parsonage and Chunky bars at the Baptist Parsonage. Then on to the Randolphs, the Quinns', the Dixons', and a dozen, two dozen more. Marty comes home with his bag of candy bulging . . . and a piece of scary, almost unbelievable knowledge.

He knows.

He knows who the werewolf is.

At one point on Marty's tour, the Beast himself, now safely between its moons of insanity, has dropped candy into his bag, unaware that Marty's face has gone deadly pale under his Don Post Yoda mask, or that, beneath his gloves, his fingers are clutching his Yoda staff so tightly that the fingernails are white. The werewolf smiles at Marty, and pats his rubber head.

But it is the werewolf. Marty knows, and not just because the man is wearing an eyepatch. There is something else— some vital similarity in this man's human face to the snarling face of the animal he saw on that silvery summer night almost four months ago now.

Since returning to Tarker's Mills from Vermont the day after Labor Day, Marty has kept a watch, sure that he will see the werewolf sooner or later, and sure that he will know him when he does because the werewolf will be a one-eyed man. Although the police nodded and said they would check it out when he told them he was pretty sure he had put out one of the were-

wolf's eyes, Marty could tell they didn't really believe him. Maybe that's because he is just a kid, or maybe it's because they weren't there on that July night when the confrontation took place. Either way, it doesn't matter. *He* knew it was so.

Tarker's Mills is a small town, but it is spread out, and until tonight Marty has not seen a one-eyed man, and he has not dared to ask questions; his mother is already afraid that the July episode may have permanently marked him. He is afraid that if he tries any out-and-out sleuthing it will eventually get back to her. Besides—Tarker's Mills is a small town. Sooner or later he will see the Beast with his human face on.

Going home, Mr. Coslaw (*Coach* Coslaw to his thousands of students, past and present) thinks Marty is so quiet because the evening and the excitement of the evening has tired him out. In truth, this is not so. Marty has never—except on the night of the wonderful bag of fireworks—felt so awake and alive. And his principal thought is this: it had taken him almost sixty days after returning home to discover the werewolf's identity because he, Marty, is a Catholic, and attends St. Mary's on the outskirts of town.

The man with the eyepatch, the man who dropped a Chunky bar into his bag and then smiled and patted him on top of his rubber head, is not a Catholic. Far from it. The Beast is the Reverend Lester Lowe, of the Grace Baptist Church.

Leaning out the door, smiling, Marty sees the eyepatch clearly in the yellow lamplight falling through the door; it gives the mousy little Reverend an almost piratical look.

"Sorry about your eye, Reverend Lowe," Mr. Coslaw said in his booming Big Pal voice. "Hope it's nothing serious?"

The Rev. Lowe's smile grew longsuffering. Actually, he said, he had lost the eye. A benign tumor; it had been necessary to remove the eye to get at the tumor. But it was the Lord's will, and he was adjusting well. He had patted the top of Marty's whole-head mask again and said that some he knew had heavier crosses to bear.

So now Marty lies in his bed, listening to the October wind sing outside, rattling the season's last leaves, hooting dimly through the eyeholes of the carven pumpkins which flank the Coslaw driveway, watching the half-moon ride the star-studded sky. The question is this: *What is he to do now?*

He doesn't know, but he feels sure that in time the answer will come.

He sleeps the deep, dreamless sleep of the very young, while outside the river of wind blows over Tarker's Mills, washing out October and bringing in cold, star-shot November, autumn's iron month.

JANUARY
FEBRUARY
MARCH
APRIL
MAY
JUNE
JULY
AUGUST
SEPTEMBER
OCTOBER
NOVEMBER
DECEMBER

The smoking butt end of the year, November's dark iron, has come to Tarker's Mills. A strange exodus seems to be taking place on Main Street. The Rev. Lester Lowe watches it from the door of the Baptist Parsonage; he has just come out to get his mail and he holds six circulars and one single letter in his hand, watching the conga-line of dusty pick-up trucks—Fords and Chevys and International Harvesters—snake its way out of town.

Snow is coming, the weatherman says, but these are no riders before the storm, bound for warmer climes; you don't head out for Florida or California's golden shore with your hunting jacket on and your gun behind you in the cab rack and your dogs in the flatbed. This is the fourth day that the men, led by Elmer Zinneman and his brother Pete, have headed out with dogs and guns and a great many six-packs of beer. It is a fad that has caught on as the full moon approaches. Bird season's over, deer season, too. But it's still open season on werewolves, and most of these men, behind the mask of their grim get-the-wagons-in-a-circle faces, are having a great time. As Coach Coslaw might has said, Doodly-damn right!

Some of the men, Rev. Lowe knows, are doing no more than skylarking; here is a chance to get out in the woods, pull beers, piss in ravines, tell jokes about polacks and frogs and niggers, shoot at squirrels and crows. *They're the real animals,* Lowe thinks, his hand unconsciously going to the eyepatch he has worn since July. *Somebody will shoot somebody, most likely. They're lucky it hasn't happened already.*

The last of the trucks drives out of sight over Tarker's Hill, horn honking, dogs yarking and barking in the back. Yes, some of the men are just skylarking, but some—Elmer and Pete Zinneman, for example—are dead serious.

If that creature, man or beast or whatever it is, goes hunting this month, the dogs will pick up its scent, the Rev. Lowe has heard Elmer say in the barber shop not two weeks ago. *And if it—or he—don't go out, then maybe we'll have saved a life. Someone's livestock at the very least.*

117

Yes, there are some of them—maybe a dozen, maybe two dozen—who mean business. But it is not them that has brought this strange new feeling into the back of Lowe's brain—that sense of being brought to bay.

It's the notes that have done that. The notes, the longest of them only two sentences long, written in a childish, laborious hand, sometimes misspelled. He looks down at the letter that has come in today's mail, addressed in that same childish script, addressed as the others have been addressed: *The Reverend Lowe, Baptist Parsonage, Tarker's Mills, Maine 04491.*

Now, this strange, trapped feeling . . . the way he imagines a fox must feel when it realizes that the dogs have somehow chased it into a cul-de-sac. That panicked moment that the fox turns, its teeth bared, to do battle with the dogs that will surely pull it to pieces.

He closes the door firmly, goes inside to the parlor where the grandfather clock ticks solemn ticks and tocks solemn tocks; he sits down, puts the religious circulars carefully aside on the table Mrs. Miller polishes twice a week, and opens his new letter. Like the others, there is no salutation. Like the others, it is unsigned. Written in the center of a sheet torn from a grade-schooler's lined notepad, is this sentence:

Why don't you kill yourself?

The Rev. Lowe puts a hand to his forehead—it trembles slightly. With the other hand he crumples the sheet of paper up and puts it in the large glass ashtray in the center of the table (Rev. Lowe does all of his counselling in the parlor, and some of his troubled parishoners smoke). He takes a book of matches from his Saturday afternoon "at home" sweater and lights the note, as he has lit the others. He watches it burn.

Lowe's knowledge of what he is has come in two distinct stages: Following his nightmare in May, the dream in which everyone in the Old Home Sunday congregation turned into a werewolf, and following his terrible discovery of Clyde Corliss's

gutted body, he has begun to realize that something is . . . well, wrong with him. He knows no other way to put it. Something *wrong*. But he also knows that on some mornings, usually during the period when the moon is full, he awakes feeling amazingly *good*, amazingly *well*, amazingly *strong*. This feeling ebbs with the moon, and then grows again with the next moon.

Following the dream and Corliss's death, he has been forced to acknowledge other things, which he had, up until then, been able to ignore. Clothes that are muddy and torn. Scratches and bruises he cannot account for (but since they never hurt or ache, as ordinary scratches and bruises do, they have been easy to dismiss, to simply . . . not think about). He has even been able to ignore the traces of blood he has sometimes found on his hands . . . and lips.

Then, on July 5th, the second stage. Simply described: he had awakened blind in one eye. As with the cuts and scratches, there had been no pain; simply a gored, blasted socket where his left eye had been. At that point the knowledge had become too great for denial: *he* is the werewolf; *he* is the Beast.

For the last three days he has felt familiar sensations: a great restlessness, an impatience that is almost joyful, a sense of tension in his body. It is coming again—the change is almost here again. Tonight the moon will rise full, and the hunters will be out with their dogs. Well, no matter. He is smarter than they give him credit for. They speak of a man-wolf, but think only in terms of the wolf, not the man. They can drive in their pickups, and he can drive in his small Volare sedan. And this afternoon he will drive down Portland way, he thinks, and stay at some motel on the outskirts of town. And if the change comes, there will be no hunters, no dogs. *They* are not the ones who frighten him.

Why don't you kill yourself?

The first note came early this month. It said simply:

I know who you are.

The second said:

120

If you are a man of God, get out of town. Go someplace where there are animals for you to kill but no people.

The third said:

End it.

That was all; just *End it.* And now

Why don't you kill yourself?

Because I don't want to, the Rev. Lowe thinks petulantly. *This— whatever it is—is nothing I asked for. I wasn't bitten by a wolf or cursed by a gypsy. It just ... happened. I picked some flowers for the vases in the church vestry one day last November. Up by that pretty little cemetery on Sunshine Hill. I never saw such flowers before ... and they were dead before I could get back to town. They turned black, every one. Perhaps that was when it started to happen. No reason to think so, exactly ... but I do. And I won't kill myself. They are the animals, not me.*

Who is writing the notes?

He doesn't know. The attack on Marty Coslaw has not been reported in the weekly Tarker's Mills newspapers, and he prides himself on not listening to gossip. Also, as Marty did not know about Lowe until Halloween because their religious circles do not touch, the Rev. Lowe does not know about Marty. And he has no memory of what he does in his beast-state; only that alcoholic sense of well-being when the cycle has finished for another month, and the restlessness before.

I am a man of God, he thinks, getting up and beginning to pace, walking faster and faster in the quiet parlor where the grandfather clock ticks solemn ticks and tocks solemn tocks. *I am a man of God and I will not kill myself. I do good here, and if I sometimes do evil, why, men have done evil before me; evil also serves the will of God, or so the Book of Job teaches us; if I have been cursed from Outside, then God will bring me down in His time. All things serve the will of God ... and who is he? Shall I make inquiries? Who was attacked on July 4th? How did I (it) lose his (its) eye? Perhaps he should be silenced ... but not this month. Let them put their dogs back in their kennels first. Yes ...*

He begins to walk faster and faster, bent low, unaware that his beard, usually scant (he can get away with only shaving once every three days ... at the right time of the month, that is), has now sprung out thick and scruffy and wiry, and that his one brown eye has gone a hazel shade that is deepening moment by moment toward the emerald green it will become later this night. He is hunching forward as he walks, and he has begun to talk to himself ... but the words are growing lower and lower, more and more like growls.

At last, as the gray November afternoon tightens down toward an early anvil-colored dusk, he bounds into the kitchen, snatches the Volare's keys from the peg by the door, and almost runs toward the car. He drives toward Portland fast, smiling, and he does not slow when the season's first snow starts to skirl into the beams of his headlights, dancers from the iron sky. He senses the moon somewhere above the clouds; he senses its power; his chest expands, straining the seams of his white shirt.

He tunes the radio to a rock and roll station, and he feels *just ... great!*

And what happens later that night might be a judgment from God, or a jest of those older gods that men worshipped from the safety of stone circles on moonlit nights—oh, it's funny, all right, pretty funny, because Lowe has gone all the way to Portland to become the Beast, and the man he ends up ripping open on that snowy November night is Milt Sturmfuller, a lifelong resident of Tarker's Mills ... and perhaps God is just after all, because if there is a first-class grade-A shit in Tarker's Mills, it is Milt Sturmfuller. He has come in this night as he has on other nights, telling his battered wife Donna Lee that he is on business, but his business is a B-girl named Rita Tennison who has given him a lively case of herpes which Milt has already passed on to Donna Lee, who has never so much as looked at another man in all the years they have been married.

The Rev. Lowe has checked into a motel called The Driftwood near the Portland-Westbrook line, and this is the same motel that Milt Sturmfuller and Rita Tennison have chosen on this November night to do their business.

Milt steps out at quarter past ten to retrieve a bottle of bourbon he's left in the car, and he is in fact congratulating himself on being far from Tarker's Mills on the night of the full moon when the one-eyed Beast leaps on him from the roof of a snow-shrouded Peterbilt ten-wheeler and takes his head off with one gigantic swipe. The last sound Milt Sturmfuller hears in his life is the werewolf's rising snarl of triumph; his head rolls under the Peterbilt, the eyes wide, the neck spraying blood, and the bottle of bourbon drops from his jittering hand as the Beast buries its snout in his neck and begins to feed.

And the next day, back in the Baptist parsonage in Tarker's Mills and feeling *just ... great*, the Rev. Lowe will read the account of the murder in the newspaper and think piously: *He was not a good man. All things serve the Lord.*

And following this, he will think: *Who is the kid sending the notes? Who was it in July? It's time to find out. It's time to listen to some gossip.*

The Rev. Lester Lowe readjusts his eyepatch, shakes out a new section of the newspaper and thinks: *All things serve the Lord, if it's the Lord's will, I'll find him. And silence him. Forever.*

123

JANUARY
FEBRUARY
MARCH
APRIL
MAY
JUNE
JULY
AUGUST
SEPTEMBER
OCTOBER
NOVEMBER
DECEMBER

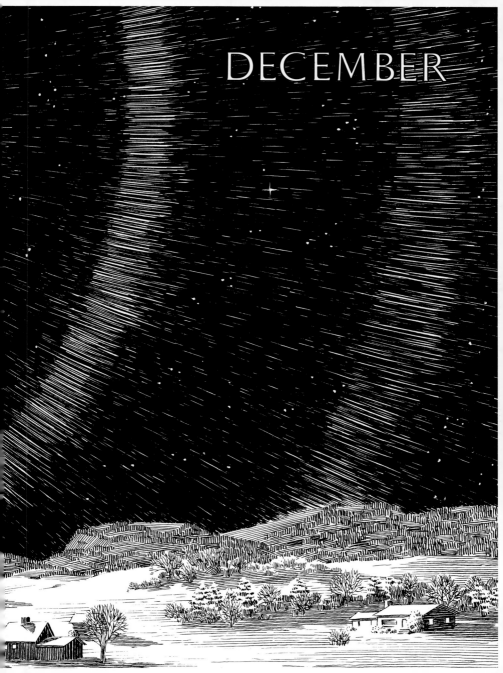

DECEMBER

It is fifteen minutes of midnight on New Year's Eve. In Tarker's Mills, as in the rest of the world, the year is drawing to its close, and in Tarker's Mills as in the rest of the world, the year has brought changes.

Milt Sturmfuller is dead and his wife Donna Lee, at last free of her bondage, has moved out of town. Gone to Boston, some say; gone to Los Angeles, other say. Another woman has tried to make a go of the Corner Bookshop and failed, but the barber shop, The Market Basket, and The Pub are doing business at the same old places, thank you very much. Clyde Corliss is dead, but his two goodfornothing brothers, Alden and Errol, are still alive and well and cashing in their foodstamps at the A&P two towns over—they don't quite have the nerve to do it right here in the Mills. Gramma Hague, who used to make the best pies in Tarker's Mills, has died of a heart attack, Willie Harrington, who is ninety-two, slipped on the ice in front of his little house on Ball Street late in November and broke his hip, but the library has received a nice bequest in the will of a wealthy summer resident, and next year construction will begin on the children's wing that has been talked about in town meeting since time out of mind. Ollie Parker, the school principal, had a nosebleed that just wouldn't quit in October and is diagnosed as an acute hypertensive. *Lucky you didn't blow your brains out*, the doctor grunted, unwrapping the blood-pressure cuff, and told Ollie to lose forty pounds. For a wonder, Ollie loses twenty of those pounds by Christmas. He looks and feels like a new man. "*Acts* like a new man, too," his wife tells her close friend Delia Burney, with a lecherous little grin. Brady Kincaid, killed by the Beast in kite-flying season, is still dead. And Marty Coslaw, who used to sit right behind Brady in school, is still a cripple.

Things change, things don't change, and, in Tarker's Mills, the year is ending as the year came in—a howling blizzard is roaring outside, and the Beast is around. Somewhere.

Sitting in the living room of the Coslaw home and watching Dick Clark's Rockin New Year's Eve are Marty Coslaw and his

Uncle Al. Uncle Al is on the couch. Marty is sitting in his wheelchair in front of the TV. There is a gun in Marty's lap, a .38 Colt Woodsman. Two bullets are chambered in the gun, and both of them are pure silver. Uncle Al has gotten a friend of his from Hampden, Mac McCutcheon, to make them in a bullet-loader. This Mac McCutcheon, after some protests, has melted Marty's silver confirmation spoon down with a propane torch, and calibrated the weight of powder needed to propel the bullets without sending them into a wild spin. "I don't guarantee they'll work," this Mac McCutcheon has told Uncle Al, "but they probably will. What you gonna kill, Al? A were-wolf or a vampire?"

"One of each," Uncle Al says, giving him his grin right back. "That's why I got you to make two. There was a banshee hanging around as well, but his father died in North Dakota and he had to catch a plane to Fargo." They have a laugh over that, and then Al says: "They're for a nephew of mine. He's crazy over movie monsters, and I thought they'd make an interesting Christmas present for him."

"Well, if he fires one into a batten, bring it back to the shop," Mac tells him. "I'd like to see what happens."

In truth, Uncle Al doesn't know what to think. He hadn't seen Marty or been to Tarker's Mills since July 3rd; as he could have predicted, his sister, Marty's mother, is furious with him about the fireworks. *He could have been killed, you stupid asshole! What in the name of God did you think you were doing?* she shouts down the telephone wire at him.

Sounds like it was the fireworks that saved his—Al begins, but there is the sharp click of a broken connection in his ear. His sister is stubborn; when she doesn't want to hear something, she won't.

Then, early this month, a call came from Marty. "I have to see you, Uncle Al," Marty said. "You're the only one I can talk to."

"I'm in the doghouse with our mom, kid," Al answered.

"It's important," Marty said. "Please. *Please."*

So he came, and he braved his sister's icy, disapproving silence, and on a cold, clear early December day, Al took Marty for a ride in his sports car, loading him carefully into the passenger bucket. Only this day there was no speeding and no wild laughter; only Uncle Al listening as Marty talked. Uncle Al listened with growing disquiet as the tale is told.

Marty began by telling Al again about the night of the wonderful bag of fireworks, and how he had blown out the creature's left eye with the Black Cat firecrackers. Then he told him about Halloween, and the Rev. Lowe. Then he told Uncle Al that he had begun sending the Rev. Lowe anonymous notes ... anonymous, that is, until the last two, following the murder of Milt Sturmfuller in Portland. Those he signed just as he had been taught in English class: *Yours truly, Martin Coslaw.*

"You shouldn't have sent the man notes, anonymous or otherwise!" Uncle Al said sharply. "Christ, Marty! Did it ever occur to you that you could be *wrong?"*

"Sure it did," Marty said. "That's why I signed my name to the last two. Aren't you going to ask me what happened? Aren't you going to ask me if he called up my father and told him I'd sent him a note saying why don't you kill yourself and another one saying we're closing in on you?"

"He didn't do that, did he?" Al asked, knowing the answer already.

"No," Marty said quietly. "He hasn't talked to my dad, and he hasn't talked to my mom, and he hasn't talked to me."

"Marty, there could be a hundred reasons for th—"

"No. There's only *one.* He's the werewolf, he's the Beast, it's *him,* and he's waiting for the full moon. As the Reverend Lowe, he can't do anything. But as the werewolf, he can do plenty. He can shut me up."

And Marty spoke with such chilling simplicity that Al was almost convinced. "So what do you want from me?" Al asked.

Marty told him. He wanted two silver bullets, and a gun to shoot them with, and he wanted Uncle Al to come over on New Year's Eve, the night of the full moon.

"I'll do no such thing," Uncle Al said. "Marty, you're a good kid, but you're going loopy. I think you've come down with a good case of Wheelchair Fever. If you think it over, you'll know it."

"Maybe," Marty said. "But think how you'll feel if you get a call on New Year's Day saying I'm dead in my bed, chewed to pieces? Do you want that on your conscience, Uncle Al?"

Al started to speak, then closed his mouth with a snap. He turned into a driveway, hearing the Mercedes' front wheels crunch in the new snow. He reversed and started back. He fought in Viet Nam and won a couple of medals there; he had successfully avoided lengthy entanglements with several lusty young ladies; and now he felt caught and trapped by his ten-year-old nephew. His *crippled* ten-year-old nephew. Of course he didn't want such a thing on his conscience—not even the *possibility* of such a thing. And Marty knew it. As Marty knew that if Uncle Al thought there was even one chance in a thousand that he might be right—

Four days later, on December 10th, Uncle Al called. "Great news!" Marty announced to his family, wheeling his chair back into the family room. "Uncle Al's coming over for New Year's Eve!"

"He certainly is *not*," his mother says in her coldest, brusquest tone.

Marty was not daunted. "Gee, sorry—I already invited him," he said. "He said he'd bring party-powder for the fireplace."

His mother had spent the rest of the day glaring at Marty every time she looked in his direction or he in hers . . . but she didn't call her brother back and tell him to stay away, and that was the most important thing.

At supper that night Katie whispered hissingly in his ear: "You *always* get what you want! Just because you're a cripple!"

Grinning, Marty whispered back: "I love you too, sis."

"You little *booger!*"

She flounced away.

And here it is, New Year's Eve. Marty's mother was sure Al wouldn't show up as the storm intensified, the wind howling and moaning and driving snow before it. Truth to tell, Marty has had a few bad moments himself... but Uncle Al arrived up around eight, driving not his Mercedes sports car but a borrowed four-wheel drive.

By eleven-thirty, everyone in the family has gone to bed except for the two of them, which is pretty much as Marty had foreseen things. And although Uncle Al is still pooh-poohing the whole thing, he has brought not one but two handguns concealed under his heavy CPO coat. The one with the two silver bullets he hands wordlessly to Marty after the family has gone to bed (as if to complete making the point, Marty's mother slammed the door of the bedroom she shares with Marty's dad when she went to bed—slammed it hard). The other is filled with more conventional lead-loads... but Al reckons that if a crazyman is going to break in here tonight (and as time passes and nothing happens, he comes to doubt that more and more), the .45 Magnum will stop him.

Now, on the TV, they are switching the cameras more and more often to the big lighted ball on top of the Allied Chemical Building in Times Square. The last few minutes of the year are running out. The crowd cheers. In the corner opposite the TV, the Coslaw Christmas tree still stands, drying out now, getting a little brown, looking sadly denuded of its presents.

"Marty, nothing—" Uncle Al begins, and then the big picture window in the family room blows inward in a twinkle of glass,

134

letting in the howling black wind from outside, twisting skirls of white snow . . . and the Beast.

Al is frozen for a moment, utterly frozen with horror and disbelief. It is huge, this Beast, perhaps seven feet tall, although it is hunched over so that its front hand-paws almost drag on the rug. Its one green eye *(just like Marty said,* he thinks numbly, *all of it, just like Marty said)* glares around with a terrible, rolling sentience . . . and fixes upon Marty, sitting in his wheelchair. It leaps at the boy, a rolling howl of triumph exploding out of its chest and past its huge yellow-white teeth.

Calmly, his face hardly changing, Marty raises the .38 pistol. He looks very small in his wheelchair, his legs like sticks inside his soft and faded jeans, his fur-lined slippers on feet that have been numb and senseless all of his life. And, incredibly, over the werewolf's mad howling, over the wind's screaming, over the clap and clash of his own tottering thoughts about how this can possibly be in a world of real people and real things, over all of this Al hears his nephew say: "Poor old Reverend Lowe. I'm gonna try to set you free."

And as the werewolf leaps, its shadow a blob on the carpet, its claw-tipped hands outstretched, Marty fires. Because of the lower powder-load, the gun makes an almost absurdly insignificant pop. It sounds like a Daisy air-rifle.

But the werewolf's roar of rage spirals up into an even higher register, a lunatic screech of pain now. It crashes into the wall and its shoulder punches a hole right through to the other side. A Currier and Ives painting falls onto its head, skates down the thick pelt of its back and shatters as the werewolf turns. Blood is pouring down the savage, hairy mask of its face, and its green eye seems rolling and confused. It staggers toward Marty, growling, its claw-hands opening and closing, its snapping jaws cutting off wads of blood-streaked foam. Marty holds the gun in both hands, as a small child holds his drinking cup.

He waits, waits . . . and as the werewolf lunges again, he fires. Magically, the beast's other eye blows out like a candle in a stormwind! It screams again and staggers, now blind, toward the window. The blizzard riffles the curtains and twists them around its head—Al can see flowers of blood begin to bloom on the white cloth—as, on the TV, the big lighted ball begins to descend its pole.

The werewolf collapses to its knees as Marty's dad, wild-eyed and dressed in bright yellow pajamas, dashes into the room. The .45 Magnum is still in Al's lap. He has never so much as raised it.

Now the beast collapses . . . shudders once . . . and dies.

Mr. Coslaw stares at it, open-mouthed.

Marty turnes to Uncle Al, the smoking gun in his hands. His face looks tired . . . but at peace.

"Happy New Year, Uncle Al," he says, "it's dead. The Beast is dead." And then he begins to weep.

On the floor, under the mesh of Mrs. Coslaw's best white curtains, the werewolf has begun to change. The hair which has shagged its face and body seems to be *pulling in* somehow. The lips, drawn back in a snarl of pain and fury, relax and cover the shrinking teeth. The claws melt magically away to finger-nails . . . fingernails that have been almost pathetically gnawed and bitten.

The Reverend Lester Lowe lies there, wrapped in a bloody shroud of curtain, snow blowing around him in random patterns.

Uncle Al goes to Marty and comforts him as Marty's dad gawks down at the naked body on the floor and as Marty's mother, clutching the neck of her robe, creeps into the room. Al hugs Marty tight, tight, tight.

"You done good, kid," he whispers. "I love you."

Outside, the wind howls and screams against the snow-filled sky, and in Tarker's Mills, the first minute of the new year becomes history.

Afterword

Any dedicated moon-watcher will know that, regardless of the year, I have taken a good many liberties with the lunar cycle—usually to take advantage of days (Valentine's, July 4th, etc.) which "mark" certain months in our minds. To those readers who feel that I didn't know any better, I assert that I did ... but the temptation was simply too great to resist.

Stephen King
August 4, 1983

SILVER BULLET

FADE IN:

1 EXT. THE FULL MOON, CLOSE NIGHT   1

It nearly fills the screen, swimming mysteriously in the warm late summer air.

SOUND: Crickets.

THE CAMERA PANS SLOWLY DOWN TO:

2 EXT. TRAIN TRACKS IN THE COUNTRY NIGHT—AND
MOONLIGHT   2

CREDITS BEGIN.

A rail-rider comes chugging along the tracks. Aboard is ARNIE WESTRUM, a big man in a strappy T-shirt and chino pants. He is drinking beer.

> ARNIE (sings)
> *My* beer is Rheingold the *dry* beer . . .
> Think of Rheingold whenever you *buy* beer . . .

He drains the rest of his own bottle of Rheingold and tosses it to one side. Up ahead we see a switching point.

ARNIE throws the rail-rider into neutral, opens the toolbox on the back, and brings out a big five-cell flashlight. He shines it on the switch.

He gets a crowbar from the toolbox, plus a big wrench, a pair of pliers, a hammer, and a pair of work gloves. He also gets another bottle of beer and sticks it into his back pocket.

ARNIE jumps down and approaches the switch.

CREDITS CONTINUE.

3 EXT. ARNIE, AT THE SWITCHING POINT NIGHT   3

He drops his tools, pulls on his work gloves, and trains the light on the switch for a moment. During this:

> ARNIE (sings)
> It's not *bitter*, not *sweet*, it's a real frosty *treat*,
> Won't you try, won't you buy Rheingold beer . . .

He tries the switch. No go. It's frozen.

NOTE: b.g., background; CU, close-up; ECU, extreme close-up; EXT, exterior; f.g., foreground; INT, interior; POV, point of view; v-o, voice-over.

ARNIE
Stuck tighter'n dogshit in a deep-freeze!

He takes the bottle of beer from his back pocket and fishes a churchkey from one of the front ones. He pops the cap and drinks deeply. He burps. Then he screws the half-empty bottle of beer into the cinders so it won't fall over. Then he picks up his crowbar.

CREDITS CONTINUE.

4 EXT.   THE RAIL-RIDER   NIGHT   4

There's a SOUND of bushes shaking. Something comes out— something *huge*. It leaps limberly onto the rail-rider. It is a werewolf with greenish-yellow eyes. Tatters of clothes still hang from it.

What kind of monster, exactly? *It* is humanoid as well as wolfish . . . and when we learn who *it* is in its human form, we should be able to spot the resemblance at once . . . and kick ourselves for not knowing earlier.

It crouches there, huge and bushy and fanged and deadly, on the whole rail-rider.

CREDITS CONCLUDE.

5 EXT.   ARNIE   NIGHT   5

He's working the crowbar into the junction point just as hard as he can. Swearing at it under his breath. Suddenly, both the tracks and the switch move.

ARNIE
Hot damn! Now . . . a little oil . . .

He turns back toward the rail-rider.

6 EXT.   ARNIE, ARRIVING AT THE RAIL-RIDER   NIGHT   6

ARNIE
It's not bitter, not sweet . . . it's a big fuckin' treat . . .

A NOISE—bushes rattling; cinders clinking and rattling. ARNIE looks around.

7 EXT.   THE RAILS AND THE SWITCHING POINT, ARNIE'S POV   7
NIGHT

Nothing there. His bottle of beer stands by the litter of his tools.

8 EXT.   ARNIE, AT THE RAIL-RIDER   NIGHT   8

He's rooting around in the toolbox, back to the switching point.

9 EXT. ARNIE'S BOTTLE OF BEER, CU NIGHT 9

A hairy hand/paw closes around it—we see huge curved claws on
that hand.

10 EXT. THE WEREWOLF'S FACE, CU NIGHT 10

Glaring green-yellow eyes; a savage, bestial face which is still half
human. That's all we see. The rest is in shadow. It opens its mouth,
and upends the bottle of beer. Foamy Rheingold begins gurgling
down the werewolf's throat.

11 EXT. ARNIE AT THE RAIL-RIDER NIGHT 11

He comes up with an old-fashioned oilcan, the kind with the long
spout. He starts back to the switching point, waving the can.

ARNIE (sings)
My beer is Rheingold the *dry* beer . . .
Think of Rheingold whenever you *fry* beer . . .

He arrives, looks down . . . and stops singing. His eyes widen.

12 EXT. THE CINDERS BY THE TRACKS, ARNIE'S POV NIGHT 12

We can see the hole where ARNIE put his beer, but it is of course
empty. Beside it are two huge prints in the cinders, half wolf, half
human.

13 EXT. ARNIE NIGHT 13

He's beginning to be afraid. Beginning to look around to see what
might be out here with him. Beginning to realize he is in extremely
deep shit.

SOUND: A SHATTERING, SNARLNG ROAR

14 EXT. THE WEREWOLF NIGHT 14

It rises up on its hind legs, eyes glaring an ugly yellow green. Its
snout wrinkles back, revealing those teeth.

15. EXT. ARNIE NIGHT 15

He's craning back to look at the thing, his face a grue of horror.

ARNIE
Oh n—

A huge clawed hand/paw comes sweeping down. ARNIE's head is
granted an immediate Reno-style divorce from the rest of his body.

16. EXT.   THE RAIL-RIDER   NIGHT   16

SOUND of the beast approaching. A hairy arm and taloned hand
reaches into the open toolbox bolted to the back and rummages. The
hand is dripping blood.

It comes up with a bottle of Rheingold.

The WEREWOLF begins to sing. It is a bizarre funny-horrible
grunting, the words hellishly recognizable:

> WEREWOLF (gutteral; subhuman)
> My beer is Rheingold the dry beer . . .

No can opener for this thing; it brings the neck of the bottle down
sharply on the edge of the toolbox. Beer foams out.

17 EXT.   THE WEREWOLF'S FACE, IN DEEP SHADOW   NIGHT   17

He/It rams the jagged neck of the bottle deep into its mouth and
drinks. Foam drizzles down its pelt. It's grinning.

> WEREWOLF (snarling voice)
> Think of Rheingold whenever you buy beer . . .

18 EXT.   THE WEREWOLF, CU   NIGHT   18

The bottle is empty. There are CRUNCHING SOUNDS as it begins to
eat the bottle.

Blood begins to run out of its mouth; its face wrinkles in pain and
fury. It spits out broken, bloody jags of glass.

Looks up. It HOWLS.

19 EXT.   TARKER'S MILLS   NIGHT—MOONLIGHT   19

We're looking at Main Street of a small country town—might be
New England, might be mid-South. Might be 1984, might be 1981.
This is Tarker's Mills, and in places like this, time moves more
slowly. Cars—not too many—move back and forth. No one is in a
hurry.

We see the Methodist church (and the parsonage next door); Andy's
Sporting Goods; Owen's Pub, with its Narragansett neon sign. We
see a barber shop with a striped pole; we see the Holy Family
Catholic Church and the rectory next door. We see the Gem Theater,
which is showing a revival of Sophia Loren in *Two Women*.

It's Our Town, U.S.A.

> JANE (voice-over)
> This place is Tarker's Mills, where I grew up . . . and
> this is how it was when I was fourteen—a place
> where people cared about each other as much as
> they cared about themselves. This is how my town

144

looked as, all unknowing, it approached the rim of
the nightmare. The killing had begun.

SOUND: The HOWL of the WEREWOLF—distant, a bit dreamy.

20 EXT./INT.   TARKER'S MILLS MONTAGE   NIGHT   20

    a.) VIRGIL CUTTS, owner of Virgil's Texaco, is filling up a car. We
        hear the HOWL . . . and VIRGIL looks up uneasily.
    b.) In the barber shop, BILLY McCLAREN, the barber, is just taking
        the apron off the Methodist minister, REV. O'BANION. They
        both look around.
    c.) Folks are coming out of the Gem Theater. They pause at the
        sound of that HOWL and look toward the edge of town.

21 EXT.   THE SETTING MOON, CU   NIGHT   21

As JANE speaks, we see the moon sink below the horizon.

JANE (v-o)
The killing had begun, but at first no one knew it.
. . . Arnie Westrum was a chronic drunk, and what
happened seemed like an accident.

22 EXT.   THE RAIL-RIDER AND ARNIE'S HEADLESS BODY
NIGHT   22

Slowly the view improves, grows lighter, as we TIME-LAPSE TO
DAWN.

SOUND: A train is approaching. We hear its horn.

CAMERA MOVES IN. Here is a shattered Rheingold bottle. There is
a litter of ARNIE'S tools. And here, on the cheek of ARNIE'S
severed head, a few ants are checking things out.

SOUND: The train's horn, MUCH CLOSER.

JANE (v-o)
The county coroner concluded that Arnie passed
out on the tracks. There wasn't enough evidence to
conclude anything else.

And suddenly the train comes smashing into the frame, horn
blaring. The rail-rider goes flying. ARNIE'S body disappears
underneath. We see something flopping and moving under there. It
could be a bundle of rags. Could be . . . but isn't.

DISSOLVE TO:

23 EXT.   TARKER'S MILLS TOWN COMMON   DAY   23

The common is more or less in the center of town, either surrounded
by Main Street commerce or backed by it. THE CAMERA MOVES
SLOWLY IN on a big tent that's been erected on the Common—
looks like a revival meeting tent, almost, but the banner draped over

the entrance reads: SUPPORT THE TARKER'S MILLS MEDCU DRIVE!

Behind or to the side, on the grass, picnic tables have been set out end-to-end. Women are putting salads and home-baked breads on these—just about the whole town is going to sit down to a meal when the meeting's over. Further off, men are tending barbecues, roasting corn, etc.

> JOE HALLER (amplified voice)
> I'd like to give you Father Lester Lowe, of Holy
> Family Catholic Church!

Enthusiastic applause greets this.

24 INT.   THE CROWD   DAY   24

Most of the town is here, seated on folding chairs. We're looking particularly at three people—NAN COSLAW, her husband BOB, and their fourteen-year-old daughter, JANE. It is JANE—a slightly older JANE—who we have heard speaking. She is now a bit bored with the meeting, which has been going on for some time. As the APPLAUSE CONTINUES, she leans toward her mother.

> JANE
> I'm going out for a while, 'kay?

> NAN
> All right. Stay close. And make sure your brother's
> all right.

As JANE gets up, the applause starts to fade a bit.

NOTE: JANE is wearing a silver crucifix, and will continue to wear it through the whole movie.

25 INT.   THE PODIUM   DAY   25

To one side is a big black-and-white photograph on an easel. It shows a van which has been customized into an emergency medical unit.

Behind the podium are four chairs. REV. TOM O'BANION sits in one of them. ANDY FAIRTON sits in another, red-faced and beaming. JOE HALLER, the town constable, is just returning to his; LESTER LOWE is just approaching the mike as the applause dies. LOWE'S face shines with love and goodwill.

> LOWE
> For the last ten years...

No amplification. He taps the mike.

26 INT.   JANE   26

She is making her way down the row to the aisle (the people should
be seated in folding chairs). She passes a GIRL of about her own age
who has overheard NAN's parting shot.

                    GIRL (mocking)
          "Make sure your brother's all right."

                    JANE (low)
          Marty's a booger.

She reaches the aisle and starts out.

27 INT.   THE PODIUM, FEATURING FATHER LOWE   27

He taps the mike again.

28 INT.   THE CROWD, FEATURING BOB AND NAN COSLAW   28

                    BOB (good-natured)
          Just pretend you're in your own church askin' for
          money, father! It'll work fine!

Good-natured laughter greets this.

29 INT.   LOWE AT THE PODIUM   29

A bit flustered, he taps the mike and is rewarded by a BRIEF
SCREAM OF FEEDBACK.

                    LOWE
          For the last ten years, I have had a dream. A dream
          of a time when modern medical care would come to
          this small community, which sometimes seems so
          far from Durham, with her lifesaving hospitals. I
          hope that this meeting, at which I see so many of
          my friends gathered, will be the start of making my
          dream come true.

SOUND: Enthusiastic applause.

30 EXT.   A SNAKE IN THE GRASS, CU   30

It's a blacksnake . . . harmless, but big. It goes wriggling through the
grass toward a stream. In the b.g.—SOUND OF APPLAUSE.

                    MARTY (voice)
          Holy . . . ! Brady, are you sure they're not
          poisonous?

                    BRADY (voice)
          Little old blacksnake? Hell, no!

Hands—the rather grimy hands of a boy bent on mischief—grab the
blacksnake.

147

31 EXT.   MARTY AND BRADY, CU   31

BRADY holds the snake up. Both boys gaze at it with respectful wonder.

NOTE: MARTY is wearing a silver St. Christopher's medallion, and will through the whole movie.

                         MARTY
              Lemme hold him!

BRADY hands it over. As MARTY looks at the snake, BRADY sees:

32 EXT.   JANE, COMING OUT OF THE TENT   DAY   32

                         JANE
              I was almost fifteen that summer. My brother Marty
              was eleven. Marty and his friend Brady Kincaid
              were the crosses I had to bear. Brady was actually
              the worse of the two, but I was rarely disposed to
              see that. Not when my younger brother was so
              constantly thrown in my face by my parents.

                         LOWE (v-o from the tent)
              $32,000 is a lot of money. But when you think of
              the lives this unit might save, it seems very
              inexpensive indeed.

Applause greets this.

33 EXT.   MARTY AND BRADY   33

Again we are fairly tight on the boys—we see them from waist or chest height. BRADY snatches back the snake.

                         BRADY
              I got an idea.

                         MARTY
              What?

BRADY looks toward JANE. MARTY follows his gaze. His eyes widen.

                         MARTY
              You wouldn't.

BRADY grins. MARTY assesses the grin.

                         MARTY
              You would.

34 INT.   THE PODIUM, WITH LOWE   34

                         LOWE
              An endeavor like this seems to me to be the very
              definition of community—all of us pulling together

as one, farmers and merchants . . . Protestants and
Catholics . . .

35 EXT.   JANE   35

She is walking slowly toward the picnic area, and is passing under a
tree. There's more applause from the tent.

BRADY (teasing voice)
Jane . . . Jane . . .

She looks up. The blacksnake dangles down toward her, almost
touching her upturned face.

JANE shrieks and bolts. She gets a little way, trips over her own feet,
and falls down hard. She's wearing what *was* a nice jumper and
nylons. Now the jumper is torn and the hose shredded at the knees.

36 EXT.   THE TREE, WITH BRADY   36

He's lying over a limb with the snake in his hand, laughing wildly.

37 EXT.   JANE   37

She gets up, looks at her clothes, her bloody knees. She's near tears.

38 EXT.   MARTY, AT ONE SIDE OF THE TREE, FAIRLY TIGHT   38

The shot's from the chest up. He looks sorry he was a part of this
little stunt, as he ought to be.

MARTY
It was just a blacksnake, Jane—

39 EXT.   JANE   39

She looks around at him in a fury of embarrassment and something
very close to hate.

JANE
Look at my knees! Look at my *dress*! *I hate you!*

40 EXT.   BRADY, UP IN THE TREE   40

BRADY
Did wittle Janey make wee-wee in her teddies?

41 EXT.   MARTY   41

MARTY
Stop it, Brady.

42 EXT.   BRADY, UP IN THE TREE   42

He throws the snake.

149

43   EXT.   JANE   43

She dodges the snake with a little scream. She's beginning to cry, but she flips BRADY the bird just the same.

44   EXT.   BRADY, IN THE TREE   44

                              BRADY
                Ooooh, *naughty!*

45   EXT.   MARTY   45

He moves toward JANE—there is something queerly unnatural in this movement, and in a moment we'll understand, but for the time being we must be puzzled.

                              MARTY
                Jane, I'm sorry. It was just a joke. We didn't
                mean—

He's reached her. JANE is sobbing now, hysterical.

                              JANE
                Oh, no! You never mean to! *I hate you, you booger!*

She runs away.

46   EXT.   THE TREE, WITH BRADY   46

He swings down and comes over to MARTY.

                              BRADY (with satisfaction)
                Really got her goat that time.

47   EXT.   MARTY   47

He's in a wheelchair, looking glumly after JANE.

                              MARTY
                Oh, shut up, Brady. You're warped.

48   EXT.   NEAR THE BANDSTAND, FEATURING JANE   DAY   48

She's walking slowly along, still crying a little. Now she steps behind some bushes, looks around, hikes up the skirt of her jumper, and wriggles out of the wrecked panty hose.

                              STELLA RANDOLPH (voice)
                Wait! Don't go!

Startled, JANE looks around, instinctively yanking her dress down. No one in sight.

                              MAN (voice; rough)
                Just leave me alone!

Now she looks toward:

49 EXT.   THE BANDSTAND, JANE'S POV   49

A man who looks like he might be a traveling salesman who has just
stepped whole and breathing from a dirty joke about the farmer's
daughter comes striding down from the bandstand.

STELLA RANDOLPH, a plump but sweetly pretty girl, comes to the
stairs but does not descend them. She is also crying—but these are
real tears, folks. STELLA is a human Niagara Falls.

                    STELLA (calls)
          Please! You have to help me!

50 EXT.   THE GAY DECEIVER   50

                    DECEIVER (keeps walking)
          It's your oven, but it ain't my bun you're baking in
          there. Sorry, babe.

B.g. SOUNDS: More applause.

51 EXT.   JANE   51

We can hear STELLA sobbing as JANE walks slowly toward the
bandstand with her panty hose still balled up in one hand. JANE
looks suddenly aware that she's not the only one in this sad world
who has troubles. She reaches the foot of the stairs going up to the
bandstand and tosses the hose absently in a litter can.

JANE mounts the steps timidly.

                    JANE
          Stella? Is that you?

52 EXT.   ON THE BANDSTAND   52

STELLA has retreated to one of the benches, where she is bawling
into a handful of Kleenex. Pudgy and twenty-two, she is both funny
and terribly sad. She looks around at the sound of JANE'S voice.

                    STELLA (alarmed)
          Who—?

                    JANE (approaching closer)
          It's Jane, Stella. Jane Coslaw.

STELLA sees it is, and turns away from her, still weeping. JANE
stands, uncertain what to do next. After a moment she approaches
closer and touches STELLA'S turned back timidly.

                    JANE (tenderly)
          What's wrong?

                    STELLA (weeping)
          He's going away. I know he is.

                          JANE
              Who's going away?

STELLA turns to her, weeping still and distracted.

                          STELLA
              What am I going to tell my *mother*? If he won't
              marry me, what am I going to tell my *mother*?

                          JANE (bewildered)
              Stella, I don't know what—

                          STELLA
              Oh, leave me alone! Just leave me *alone*, you stupid
              thing!

STELLA lumbers across the bandstand and down the steps. JANE
stares after her, bewildered and perhaps even a little frightened.

53   INT.   THE PODIUM, WITH REV. O'BANION   53
                          O'BANION
              Let us pray.

54   INT.   THE TOWN HALL GATHERING   54

Most of them bow their heads.

55   INT.   REV. O'BANION, AT THE PODIUM   55
                          O'BANION
              May the Grace of God shine upon these gathered
              here . . . and lift them up . . . and grant success to the
              endeavor to which they have so openheartedly
              declared their support. Amen.

56   INT.   THE GATHERING   56

They raise their heads. Some echo the "Amen." Others cross
themselves.

57   EXT.   THE PICNIC AREA   57

People are coming out and getting ready to chow-down.

58   EXT.   THE COSLAW STATION WAGON   DAY   58

Traveling along a country road. Headed home.

59   INT.   THE STATION WAGON   DAY   59

BOB and NAN COSLAW are sitting up front. MARTY and JANE are
in the backseat. JANE is as far from MARTY as she can get. She's
still mad as hell. Band-Aids crisscross her knees.

MARTY'S wheelchair is collapsed in the cargo area of the wagon.

NAN turns around to look at the kids—and it's really JANE she's mad at.

> NAN
> I want you two to bury the hatchet. You're being very silly, Jane.

> JANE (hot)
> Did you see my *knees*?

> MARTY
> Jane, I—

> NAN
> I think you're being *mean* as well as silly. Your brother has never had a scraped knee in his whole *life*.

Well, here it is—the chief source of JANE'S animus against her brother and the source of most of the tension in the COSLAW family.

MARTY winces and turns away a little, embarrassed—this always happens. He doesn't like it, but he doesn't know how to make his parents—his mother in particular—quit it.

> JANE
> You always take his side because he's a cripple! Well, it's not *my* fault that he's a cripple!

> MARTY
> Come on, Jane—it was Brady's idea. I couldn't stop him.

> JANE
> Brady's a booger and so are you!

> NAN
> *Jane Coslaw!*

> BOB (roars)
> *Stop it or I'll throw the whole bunch of you out!*

In this traditional family unit, BOB is the Voice of Authority. They all heed, although the atmosphere remains thundery.

60 INT.   THE STATION WAGON   DAY   60

Train tracks run near the road.

61 INT.   THE STATION WAGON, ENSEMBLE   DAY   61

> BOB (points)
> That's where poor old Arnie Westrum pitched his last drunk.

He crosses himself and they all look toward:

153

62 EXT.   THE GS&WM RAILROAD TRACKS (STATION WAGON'S   62
    POV)

63 INT.   THE CAR   DAY   63

                            BOB
          They had to pick up what was left of him in a
          peach basket.

                            JANE
          Oh, Daddy! *Gross!*

                            MARTY
          Did he really get his head cut off, Dad? That's what
          Brady said.

                            JANE
          If you don't stop it I'm going to vomit. I mean it.

                            NAN (no sympathy)
          You're not going to vomit, Jane. And I think we've
          all had quite enough of this horror-movie talk.

64 INT.   MARTY, CLOSER   DAY   64

    Craning back to look at the spot where ARNIE bit the dust. His face
    is thoughtful, solemn.

                        DISSOLVE TO:

65 EXT.   THE COSLAW HOUSE   NIGHT   65

    Lights on downstairs and upstairs.

                            NAN (voice)
              Go on, you two! Go to bed!

    One of the lights goes off upstairs.

66 INT.   JANE'S BEDROOM   NIGHT   66

    JANE is lying in bed, her face to the wall. Dim light falls on her
    unhappy face as the door is opened.

                            MARTY (v-o)
              Janey? . . . Are you awake?

    JANE says nothing.

67 INT.   THE DOOR TO JANE'S BEDROOM, WITH MARTY   67
    NIGHT

    He is in his "house wheelchair"—not the Silver Bullet (he was in the
    Bullet during the Common scene, but we didn't get a very good look
    at it). He has some stuff on his lap. A box, for sure.

MARTY

Can I come in?

68 INT. JANE   68

Her eyes are open but she says nothing. Just looks at the wall.

69 INT. MARTY   69

He rolls across to her bed and puts something on her night table.
SOUND of change and a rattle of paper. She rolls over and sees he's
put about three bucks on the table. Plus a can of mixed nuts.

JANE

What's the money for?

MARTY

A new pair of panty hose. Is it enough?

JANE

I don't want your money. You're a booger.

MARTY

It was Brady's idea, Jane. Honest to God. Please
take the money. I want to make up.

She looks at him and sees he's sincere—honestly contrite. She
softens. There's hope for these two kids yet, maybe.

JANE

I can get a pair of L'Eggs down at the pharmacy for
a dollar forty-nine. Here.

She pushes the rest back to him, then looks at the can. She picks it
up, curious.

MARTY

That's for you, too. Uncle Al gave it to me—

JANE (scorn)

That drunk!

MARTY

—but I want you to have it.

He gives her a warm, melting smile. When your little brother is
being good to you it's time to watch out—but JANE has been lulled.
She starts to open it, then looks questioningly at him.

MARTY

Yeah, go ahead.

She opens it. A long paper snake—the kind with a spring inside it—
leaps out. She shrieks.

155

JANE

You booger!

MARTY backs up the wheelchair so he's out of her reach.

MARTY (grinning)
It really *is* for your birthday, though—try it on
Brady. He'll wet his pants.

JANE
Go to hell!

70 INT.   MARTY, BY THE DOOR   70

MARTY (smiling)
I love you, Janey.

71 INT.   JANE, IN BED   71

She tries to be angry with him . . . and cannot (this is a response,
we'll find, that both MARTY and his UNCLE AL evoke). She smiles
at him a little.

72 INT.   MARTY   72

He reverses his wheelchair, also smiling a little, and leaves.

73 EXT.   TARKER'S MILLS, UNDER THE MOON   NIGHT   73

We're looking down at a brave little nestle of lights.

SOUND: A HOWL.

74 EXT.   A HOUSE SOME DISTANCE OUT IN THE COUNTRY   74

There's one light on upstairs and another downstairs . . . also
downstairs is the bluish flicker of TV light.

An ivy trellis climbs one side of the house.

SOUNDS: Canned laughter; TV dialogue.

75 INT.   THE LIVING ROOM OF THE RANDOLPH HOUSE   75

STELLA'S MOTHER, asleep in front of the TV.

76 INT.   A PRETTY CHINA DISH, CU   76

A whole bunch of capsules are dumped into it.

THE CAMERA DRAWS BACK to show us STELLA, sitting by her
vanity mirror. The rest of the room is reflected in the mirror,
including the window—we are upstairs.

[NOTE: It would be nice to see that fat moon floating in the
window!]

There's a framed picture of STELLA's ex-boyfriend on the vanity beside the dish of pills. STELLA sets down the empty prescription bottle the pills came from beside this picture. We can clearly read the word *Nembutol* on it. There is also a large glass of water on the vanity table.

STELLA turns the picture facedown. She might be crying but probably she's not. She takes about five of the pills, starts to lift them to her mouth—

A HOWL outside . . . closer.

STELLA looks around for a moment, then takes the pills with some water. She pauses, looking at herself.

> STELLA
> Suicides go to hell. Especially if they're pregnant.
> And I don't even care.

She takes another five pills. And another five.

SOUNDS: Rattling foliage.

77 EXT.   THE IVY TRELLIS   NIGHT   77

Claw-hands are seizing it and climbing. SOUNDS of hoarse, guttural breathing.

78 INT.   STELLA AT THE VANITY TABLE   78

She takes another handful of pills . . . and the window behind her shatters inward. There is a bellowing roar as the werewolf throws itself through.

79 INT.   THE LIVING ROOM, WITH MOTHER   79

She sits up, startled awake.

From upstairs: ANOTHER SHATTERING ROAR . . . FOLLOWED BY A SCREAM.

80 INT.   STELLA'S ROOM, WITH STELLA   80

She runs . . . and a huge claw-hand rips through the back of her nightgown.

81 INT.   THE LIVING ROOM, WITH MOTHER   81

> MOTHER
> Oh my dear God . . . Stella!

She runs for the doorway and the hall. From upstairs comes a confusion of SOUNDS: roars, breaking furniture, shattering glass.

82 INT.   STELLA'S BED, CU   82

One of those deadly claw-hands sweeps down the bed, ripping
through the sheets . . . the mattress . . . the spring itself.

Hairy, muddy feet with protruding talons leap onto it.

83 EXT.   STELLA'S WINDOW, EXTREME UP-ANGLE   83

The werewolf leaps out—it's graceful, savage, animal.

SOUND: A TRIUMPHANT HOWL.

84 INT.   THE UPSTAIRS HALL, WITH MOTHER   84

She's found an ancient pistol somewhere and is lugging it gamely
along.

MOTHER
Stella! . . . Stella!

She reaches the closed door of STELLA's room, vacillates there for a
moment . . . and then pushes it open and goes in.

A long beat of silence while we hold on the door.

MOTHER SHRIEKS.

85 INT.   MOTHER'S FACE, ECU   85

She shrieks again.

86 INT.   STELLA'S ROOM, WIDE   86

It's a total shambles; blood is splattered everywhere; the mirror is
broken, the picture of DAN the gay deceiver is broken; the bed is
torn in two. There are big, muddy wolfprints on the remains of the
bed.

STELLA lies propped in the corner with Nembutols all around her.
Suicide may have been what she planned, but it sure isn't what
happened.

MOTHER SHRIEKS

87 EXT.   TARKER'S MILLS MONTAGE   MORNING   87

a.) MR. PELTZER puts out his paper rack—just the *Press-Herald* this
    morning. He looks shocked and grim. The scare headline:
    BRUTAL MURDER ROCKS WESTERN MAINE. We can see STELLA'S
    photograph.
b.) Through the window of Robertson's Luncheonette, we see the
    proprietor, BOBBY ROBERTSON, talking earnestly with a bunch
    of men. Among them: MILT STURMFULLER, ALFIE
    KNOPFLER, VIRGIL CUTTS, BILLY McCLAREN, and ELMER
    ZINNEMAN, a farmer we'll meet later.

c.) At Andy's Spring Goods, ANDY FAIRTON is putting a big hand-lettered sign in the window. It reads: REMINGTON SHOTGUNS SINGLE ACTION DOUBLE ACTION PUMP PROTECT YOURSELF AND YOUR FAMILY!

d.) At the Methodist parsonage, a '53 Dodge pulls slowly out and MOTHER RANDOLPH gets out, weeping. As she approaches the parsonage door, LESTER LOWE comes out and embraces her.

88 EXT.   A SMALL BRICK BUILDING ON MAIN STREET   88

The sign reads: TARKER'S MILLS TOWN OFFICE.

89 INT.   A HALLWAY, FEATURING A DOOR WITH A PEBBLED-   89
GLASS PANEL

Neatly lettered on the panel; TARKER'S MILLS CONSTABULARY. And below this: JOSEPH HALLER.

> JOE HALLER (voice)
> Okay . . . yes . . . Oh, fuck off!!

90 INT.   THE CONSTABLE'S OFFICE, WITH HALLER AND PETE   90
SYLVESTER

HALLER slams the phone down with an angry bang. He looks like a guy who has been up all night. PETE, his pudgy deputy, looks like a high school athlete who has suddenly found himself batting in the World Series.

> PETE
> What'd they say, Joe?

> HALLER
> They said they'd be here by noon.

> PETE (nervous)
> Maybe it wasn't such a good idea telling that
> Smokey Bear from the Detective Division to fuck
> off, Joe.

> HALLER (morosely)
> I waited until he hung up. Jesus, what a mess. I
> wish I'd stayed in the army. Let's go on out there.

He gets slowly up.

91 EXT.   TARKER'S MILLS CONSOLIDATED SCHOOL   91
AFTERNOON

It's a comfortable red-brick building on a side street. Ivy climbs up the sides. Two or three rows of bikes stand along one side of the building.

SOUND: The bell rings.

A beat or two, then the doors bang wide and a billion kids spill out. It's the end of the first day of school, and they are excited. They range from Grade 1 to Grade 8. Most kids book it for home as fast as they can, getting on their bikes and riding or just running.

Everyone has a pink report card.

92 EXT.   A BUNCH OF KIDS, WITH BRADY KINCAID AND TAMMY   92
STURMFULLER

BRADY and TAMMY are riding bikes. Now there is the SOUND of a gasoline engine, and MARTY catches up. He's got the Silver Bullet's motor running for the first time in the movie. Later on it will sound extremely powerful, like a racing car, but now it just sounds like a big lawnmower engine with a muffler on it. It's pretty cool, though—a bright metallic silver with flame decals on the motor housing. Looks sort of like something Big Daddy Roth might have thought up. On the back is a license plate which says SILVER BULLET.

                    BRADY
          Look out! Look out! It's Madman Marty and the
          Silver Bullet!

TAMMY laughs.

                    BRADY
          You glad to be back in jail, Marty?

                    MARTY
          Sure—I like school.

                    TAMMY
          You booger.

                    MARTY
          That's what my sister says, too. Pretty soon I'm
          going to start checking the mirror to see if I'm
          turning green.

                    BRADY
          I gotta split—see ya, Marty . . . Tammy.

93 EXT.   THE CORNER OF MAIN AND WALNUT, A WIDER SHOT   93
AFTERNOON

TAMMY and MARTY watch as BRADY zooms off toward home on his bike. MARTY pushes in a hand clutch and moves a small lever. He bumps down over the curb and they cross the street side by side, TAMMY on her bike, MARTY in his wheelchair.

94 EXT.   MARTY AND TAMMY FROM THE FAR CURB, REVERSE   94

He pops up over the curbing with a bounce. He shoves in the little hand clutch and revs the engine. *Va-room!*

160

Though Marty Coslaw (Corey Haim) is only a young, frightened boy in a wheelchair, he is out to stop the killer who is threatening Tarker's Mills.

Jane Coslaw (Megan Follows), Marty's sister, resents the attention Marty gets, but she unites with him to stop the killer.

Uncle Red (Gary Busey) is a favorite with the children. He builds a special motorized wheelchair that Marty calls the Silver Bullet.

Nan Coslaw (Robin Groves) thinks her brother Red is a bad influence on Marty and doesn't hesitate to say so.

Joe Haller (Terry O'Quinn), the Sheriff, tries to stop a lynch mob out to find the killer. . . .

The mob is unprepared for the real enemy—a werewolf.

Reverend Lowe (Everett McGill) comforts his parishioners after Marty's young friend is killed.

Reverend Lowe's congregation seem to be transformed before his very eyes—they are all werewolves!

The parishioners carouse in church...

...and attack Reverend Lowe.

After Marty has sneaked out of the house, he realizes that he is about to confront the werewolf.

Reverend Lowe wants to kill Marty when Marty learns his terrible secret.

The werewolf, intent on killing Marty, crashes into the Coslaws' house.

Marty and Jane, armed only with one silver bullet, confront the werewolf.

                    MARTY
Not bad, huh? My Uncle Al took off the regular
muffler and put on a Cherry Bomb.

                    TAMMY
What's that?

                    MARTY
Glasspack. He said he'd come over sometime this
summer and we'd soup up the engine . . . but now I
dunno. He's getting a divorce and he's in the
doghouse with my mother.

                    TAMMY
For getting a divorce?

                    MARTY
Well . . . it *is* his third.

95 EXT.   A STREET ON THE OUTSKIRTS OF TOWN, WITH MARTY   95
    AND TAMMY

The other kids are gone; they are alone. The sidewalk has ended and
they roll slowly along the dirt verge of the road. They look toward:

96 EXT.   THE RANDOLPH HOUSE, MARTY AND TAMMY'S POV   96

The driveway is blocked off with a sawhorse bearing the stenciled
words POLICE INVESTIGATION. The yard is filled with cop cars—
HALLER'S constable car, plus a number of state police vehicles.
Uniformed men come and go.

We can see a large black wreath on the door.

97 EXT.   MARTY AND TAMMY   97

                    TAMMY
Thanks for coming with me, Marty—I was scared
to go past her house by myself.

                MARTY (matter-of-fact)
Yeah . . . it *is* a little scary.

                    TAMMY
I mean, I *saw* her. All the time.

TAMMY stops her bike. She's on the verge of tears.

                    TAMMY
I used to see her *every day,* and she never knew
what was going to happen to her, and neither did I!
I mean I know how stupid that sounds, but . . .

                    MARTY
Hey, take it easy. I know how you feel.

He gets the Silver Bullet moving again, and she has to pedal along to catch up.

98 EXT.   THE STURMFULLER DRIVEWAY, WITH MARTY AND   98
TAMMY

They stop at the end.

> TAMMY
> There's something else scary.

> MARTY
> What?

> TAMMY (points)
> That.

99 EXT.   OLD GREENHOUSE, MARTY AND TAMMY'S POV   99

It stands a bit behind the house itself. A creepy place. Many of the glass panes are broken; some of these—not many—have been blocked with cardboard. The inside is a jungle of plants that have run to riot. In the f.g. is a mucky-looking garden patch where nothing much is growing.

100 EXT.   MARTY AND TAMMY   100

She is quite deeply troubled.

> TAMMY
> I've been hearing noises in there.

> MARTY
> What kind of noises?

> TAMMY
> Rattling. Rustling.

> MARTY
> Rats . . .

> TAMMY
> And my dad says it's kids. But it's not rats and it's not kids. It's—

101 EXT.   THE STURMFULLER HOUSE, WITH MILT   101

Oh my suds and body, here is the Great American Alcoholic for sure—the rural version. MILT is wearing a suit of pee-stained thermal underwear. He's wearing a baseball cap with the word *Caterpillar* on the front and has a bottle of beer in one hand (I'm pretty sure that his beer is Rheingold the dry beer). With his other hand he is busily scratching his crotch.

MILT
Tammy, you get on in here and do some dishes!

102 EXT.   THE GREENHOUSE   102

Sinister . . . spooky.

TAMMY (voice)
I've got to go.

103 EXT.   MARTY AND TAMMY   103

MARTY
I'd go out and take a look myself, but I think the
Bullet'd get stuck in the garden. It looks sorta
greasy.

She smiles at him, bends over, and kisses him on the mouth.
MARTY is stunned . . . but happy.

TAMMY
You would, wouldn't you?

MARTY (Joe Cool)
Sure. No sweat.

TAMMY
Well, it's probably nothing. I'm just spooked since
. . . you know.

MARTY
Yeah . . . but if you hear any more noises, tell your
father. Okay?

TAMMY
Okay. Have you got enough gas to get home,
Marty?

MARTY (Startled)
Jeez!

104 EXT.   THE WHEELCHAIR "DASHBOARD," MARTY'S POV   104

There's a gas gauge here, and the needle is almost on *E.*

105 EXT.   MARTY AND TAMMY   105

MARTY
I'm *always* doing this! I gotta go, Tammy.

MILT (voice)
TAMMY!

TAMMY (calls)
Coming Daddy! (To MARTY) Bye . . . thanks again for
coming home with me.

171

She waves and goes biking down the driveway as MARTY motors
back onto the street and turns toward town.

106 EXT.   TAMMY   106

She brings her bike to a stop by her father.

>   MILT
> 'Bout time. Why you want to hang around that
> cripple?

>   TAMMY
> I like him.

>   MILT
> Goddamn cripples always end up on welfare.
> Ought to electrocute all of 'em. Balance the fucking
> budget.

Having delivered this pearl of wisdom, MILT goes inside, now
scratching his ass. TAMMY pauses a moment and looks toward THE
CAMERA, her face troubled and scared.

107 EXT.   THE DESERTED GREENHOUSE, TAMMY'S VIEW   107

>   DISSOLVES TO:

108 EXT.   MARTY   108

He's buzzing along toward downtown, which is still some distance
away—but at least he's made it back to the sidewalk again.

>   MARTY (prayerfully)
> Come on, baby—

He looks down at:

109 EXT.   THE WHEELCHAIR GAS GAUGE, MARTY'S POV   109

Now the needle is lying all the way over on E.

110 EXT.   VIRGIL'S TEXACO   LATE AFTERNOON   110

MARTY pulls in. The wheelchair motor starts to pop and lug and
misfire. The chair makes it to the first pump on the island closest to
the street and then stalls as VIRGIL CUTTS comes over.

>   VIRGIL
> Well, Marty! I see you lucked out again!

>   MARTY
> Yep. Would you fill it up, please, Mr. Cutts?

>   VIRGIL
> Want me to check the oil?

                    MARTY
        Sure!

                    VIRGIL
        Wipe the windshield an check the driver's bullshit
        level?

MARTY laughs; VIRGIL starts carefully pumping gas into the Silver
Bullet's small tank.

111 EXT.   THE COSLAW HOUSE   NIGHT   111

Overhead is the moon, three days past the full.

                    UNCLE AL (voice)
        I'll see your Carlton Fiske and raise you a George
        Brett...a Dave Kingman...and a Rod Carew.

112 INT.   THE KITCHEN DOORWAY, WITH NAN COSLAW   NIGHT   112

She's wiping her hands with a dishtowel and looks like she just bit
into a lemon.

113 INT.   THE DEN, WITH UNCLE AL AND MARTY   NIGHT   113

UNCLE AL is the family's sheep of a darker color. He's thirty, good-
looking, raffish. He's also drunk. He's got both whiskey and beer.
An ashtray beside him overflows with butts.

He and MARTY are playing draw poker for MARTY'S baseball cards.
Each has a pile in front of him.

MARTY really loves UNCLE AL...his eyes just glow when he looks
at him.

                    MARTY
        Okay, okay. I call.

He tosses in three baseball cards.

                    UNCLE AL
        Wait a minute, wait a minute!

He grabs one of MARTY'S cards, looks at it, and tosses it back.

                    UNCLE AL
        Ralph Houk! You can't bet a *manager*! Stone the
        crows!

                    MARTY
        Okay, okay. Dwight Evans.

                    UNCLE AL
        Piss on him. Piss on *all* the Red Sox.

He swallows whiskey and chases it with beer.

                              173

114 INT. THE DEN, A WIDER ANGLE   114

NAN comes briskly over. She's seen and heard enough. She favors
UNCLE AL with a glare and then looks protectively at MARTY.

                        NAN
            Come on, Marty—bedtime.

She starts to wheel him away.

                        MARTY
        Mom—!

                        UNCLE AL
            Let the boy finish the game, Nan.

He means it, drunk or not. She reluctantly rolls MARTY back to the
table.

                        NAN
            Make it quick.

UNCLE AL lays down his hand.

                        UNCLE AL
            Three kings.

                        MARTY (delighted)
            I got a straight to the queen!

                        UNCLE AL
            Bullshit luck!

                        NAN (outraged)
            That's *enough*!

                        MARTY (as his mother wheels him away)
            Aww, Mom—!

115 INT. THE STAIRWELL OF THE COSLAW HOME   115

MARTY is sitting in a stair chair that rises slowly to the second floor.
He looks dejected and glum.

SOUND of NAN hectoring her brother AL. I don't think we can
make out all of what's going on, but we've all known women like
NAN and I think we can fill in the blanks. "Christian household...
you come here drunk and expect...can't even bother to call
ahead..." Etc., etc.

A wheelchair stands on the second-floor landing. This one is no
Silver Bullet, only the more humble sort that moves by arm power.
When the stair chair clicks to a stop, MARTY hoists himself from it
into the wheelchair and rolls down the hall toward the bathroom.

Below, NAN'S rant is still going on.

174

116 INT.   THE DEN, WITH NAN AND UNCLE AL   NIGHT   116

UNCLE AL is clearing up in a kind of drunken stupor—and I mean
he is *really* drunk. He's smoking one cigarette; another is smoldering
away in the heaping ashtray. He drops a pile of baseball cards on the
floor and bonks his head on the table bending down to pick them
up.

                    NAN
        I don't want you drinking around Marty. That's too
        much. If you can't stop it, you better stay away.

AL straightens up. There is a sort of command force in this man,
and here he is partly able to rise above his abysmal drunkenness so
we can see it.

                    UNCLE AL
        I come here because Marty needs a friend.

                    NAN
        Yes . . . you've always been that to him. But if you
        can't leave your booze in whatever dump you call
        home, you better just stay away.

She leaves the room, almost crying. UNCLE AL looks after her, and
then his attention is drawn to the smoldering ashtray. He pours beer
over the mess, putting out the fire but creating something that looks
even worse. He begins drunkenly picking up again.

                    UNCLE AL (to himself)
        Another wonderful time at Sister Nan's house!
        Heeyyy!

117 INT.   THE UPSTAIRS COSLAW BATHROOM   117

MARTY, now in pj's, is brushing his teeth.

JANE comes in—she's wearing a nightie.

                    MARTY
        Mom was really mad at him this time, wasn't she?

                    JANE
        What do you expect, when he comes in smelling
        like a brewery and looking like an unmade bed?

                    MARTY
        Stop it!

He lunges at her, but JANE steps back easily. MARTY overbalances
and falls out of the wheelchair. His toothbrush clatters across the tile.

                    BOB COSLAW (sleepy voice)
        Hey! That you, Marty?

                        175

JANE
He's okay, Dad!

She looks around swiftly, then bends down.

118 INT.   MARTY AND JANE, A MUCH CLOSER SHOT   118

One of MARTY'S cheeks is pressed against the floor. His eyes are
shut. He's weeping.

JANE (low)
Marty, are you all right?

MARTY
Yes. Go away.

JANE
Let me help you up.

NAN (voice)
Marty?

SOUND of her climbing the stairs.

JANE throws a quick look back over her shoulder and then helps
MARTY up in his chair. He helps by pulling on the sink counter.
JANE has time to give MARTY one quick look—"Please don't tell on
me," it says.

NAN comes in.

NAN
Jane, have you been teasing your brother again?

MARTY
She wasn't, Mom—I dropped my toothbrush and
fell over when I tried to get it. Jane helped pick me
up.

He bats his eyes at her.

MARTY (syrupy voice)
Jane's *wunnnderful*.

JANE picks up his toothbrush.

JANE (hands it to him)
Here. Brush them good, Marty. Some of that shit in
your head might leak down into your mouth and
poison you.

NAN
Jane Coslaw!

But JANE stalks off. MARTY is grinning. It was a good put-down.

119 EXT.   THE STURMFULLER HOUSE   NIGHT   119

We can see the moon in the sky beyond the ruined greenhouse.

THE CAMERA MOVES SLOWLY TOWARD the greenhouse. We begin to pick up SOUNDS: RATTLING . . . RUSTLING . . . and low animal GRUNTS.

120 INT.   TAMMY'S BEDROOM   NIGHT   120

She's deeply asleep.

121 INT.   THE LIVING ROOM   NIGHT   121

"Big-time Wrestling" on the TV. SOUND of a refrigerator door closing. MILT STURMFULLER comes into the living room from the kitchen. He's wearing his long johns with the designer pee stains and has a quart bottle of Rheingold the dry beer in each hand. He sits down, looking at the TV.

                    MILT (drunk)
         Give him the airplane! Wring his neck!

122 EXT.   THE GREENHOUSE   NIGHT   122

More noises. There is a beat of silence, and then something—one of those earthen plant pots, I think—falls over and SHATTERS.

123 INT.   THE LIVING ROOM, WITH MILT   123

He looks up briefly—he's heard something—but the crowd on the TV is loud and the match is reaching its climax.

                    MILT (all eyes again)
         Give him the sleeper, you fuckin bugwit!

124 EXT.   THE GREENHOUSE, CLOSER   124

A LOW SNARL. Plants shake and shiver. Another crash, LOUDER.

125 INT.   MILT, IN THE LIVING ROOM   125

Looks toward the window. He gets up, goes over, and looks out.

126 EXT.   THE GREENHOUSE, MEDIUM-LONG (MILT'S POV)   126

SOUND of another crash. Plants move.

127 INT.   THE HALL, WITH MILT   127

He takes a shotgun from the wall, breaks it, and looks inside.

                    MILT
         Let's see if you want to come back and break my
         pots all to shit after I put some rock salt in your
         asses!

128 INT.   THE STURMFULLER GREENHOUSE   NIGHT   128

The door at the end SCREECHES OPEN and MILT, still holding the shotgun at port arms, comes cautiously in. This place is *really* overgrown.

MILT advances slowly into the jungle of plants, and the director will shoot it as he likes to build the suspense. I'm sure that plants brush his face, and a bug or two—maybe even a big plump spider—will land on him.

He hears a SCUTTERING SOUND and whirls.

>   MILT (shouts)
>   Who's there?

129 INT.   GREENHOUSE FLOOR, MILT'S POV   NIGHT   129

A mouse goes running across the warped boards (which have pulled apart from each other, showing deep cracks between).

130 INT.   MILT   NIGHT   130

He relaxes and starts forward again. We keep expecting *it* to happen, but *it* keeps *not* happening.

Then, as MILT is starting back toward the door, two big, hairy arms come up *through the floor*—bursting through two of those cracks and shoving the splintered boards upward—and grab MILT'S legs at the knees.

SOUNDS: BESTIAL ROARS.

MILT screams and triggers off the shotgun—unfortunately, it is pointing straight up. Glass showers down on him. He is pulled down into the shattered hole—now we can see him only from the knees up.

131 INT.   TAMMY STURMFULLER'S BEDROOM   131

She sits up in bed.

SOUNDS of ROARS and MILT SCREAMING from the greenhouse.

MRS. STURMFULLER, in a nightgown with her hair done up in rollers, comes into Tammy's room.

>   MRS. STURMFULLER
>   Tammy, where's your father?

SOUND: Another SCREAM from the greenhouse.

132 INT.   THE GREENHOUSE, WITH MILT   132

He's now waist deep in the hole in the floor, surrounded by broken, splintered boards.

SOUNDS: RIPPING FLESH, CRUNCHING BONES. MILT SHRIEKS.

He is abruptly jerked downward again. He is being eaten from the feet up. As he's jerked down, one of the leaning, splintered boards rams into his chest. MILT collapses over it like an old Roman collapsing on his sword.

A hairy arm reaches up and grabs his neck. MILT is jerked all the way into the hole, board and all.

133 EXT.   THE GREENHOUSE, FROM TAMMY'S BEDROOM
      WINDOW   133

      SOUNDS of SNARLS, GROWLS, GRUNTS.

134 INT.   TAMMY AND MRS. STURMFULLER   134

      They are hugging each other, terrified, by the window.

135 EXT.   THE STURMFULLER PLACE, MEDIUM-LONG   DAY   135

      The police cars are now *here*. There's also a meat wagon. As we watch, a number of cops—JOE HALLER and PETE SYLVESTER are among them—approach the wagon. Many are carrying canvas bags.

136 EXT.   THE STURMFULLER YARD, FEATURING PETE SYLVESTER   136

      He drops the blood stained bag he's carrying, runs to the bushes, and noisily blows his groceries.

137 EXT.   TARKER'S MILLS MONTAGE #3   DUSK   137

      a.) On Oak Street, MRS. THAYER is hurrying toward home, obviously spooked. She keeps looking behind herself and nearly flies up the steps to her house. Then there is the endless business of fumbling with her keys. Finally she lurches inside and slams the door.
      b.) On Main Street, at the Holy Family rectory, FATHER O'BANION is closing the shutters . . . and locking them.
      c.) On a residential street, a kid is playing with some plastic trucks outside of a picket fence. Except for him, the street is deserted. His mother comes out and hauls him in.
      d.) ANDY FAIRTON, in the sporting-goods store, checks an automatic pistol and then holsters it on his hip. He has a pugnacious, unpleasant look.
      e.) BILLY McCLAREN turns the sign on the door of his barber shop from OPEN to CLOSED, looks out warily at the street (to make sure there are no psycho killers out there waiting for trims, I guess), then leaves and locks the door behind him. THE CAMERA FOLLOWS him down a couple of store fronts to Alfie's, where he also goes in.

f.) The paper rack in front of Peltzer's Drug. The *Press-Herald* headline is a sixteen-pointer: MANIAC CLAIMS 2ND VICTIM.

138 EXT. MARTY AND BRADY KINCAID MAGIC HOUR 138

They're flying kites on the common. Some distance in the b.g. is the bandstand. MARTY is of course flying his kite as he sits in the Silver Bullet. The boys are having a blast.

THE CAMERA SLOWLY MOVES AWAY from the boys, centers on Owen's Pub across the street, and ZOOMS IN.

In the window is a poster. It reads: $10,000 REWARD FOR INFORMATION LEADING TO THE CAPTURE OF THE MAN (OR ANIMAL) WHO KILLED STELLA RANDOLPH AND MILTON STURMFULLER. And, at the bottom: TARKER'S MILLS CITIZENS' COMMITTEE.

Along comes ANDY FAIRTON. He goes into the pub.

139 INT. ALFIE'S PUB 139

At a f.g. table: VIRGIL CUTTS, BOBBY ROBERTSON, ELMER ZINNEMAN, and his brother PORTER ZINNEMAN. Behind them, at the bar, we see PETE SYLVESTER having a beer with BILLY McCLAREN. As we look around the bar, we will also see FATHER LESTER LOWE, sitting at an unobtrusive corner table, nursing a beer and listening closely to the conversation.

> ELMER (to VIRGIL)
> Don't tell *me* an animal can't rip a man up the way Milt Sturmfuller was ripped up!

> VIRGIL
> But the woman's bed was ripped *right down the middle*, Elmer—it'd take a chainsaw to do something like that!

> PORTER
> Damn straight!

> ELMER
> Shut up, Porter. (To VIRGIL) What about the tracks?

ANDY FAIRTON has joined the group. He sits down uninvited.

> VIRGIL
> That could be something to throw off the cops. And it ain't *animals* that try to confuse the law; it's *people* do that.

> ANDY FAIRTON
> Law around here don't *need* much confusing.

PETE looks around at this. Being the deputy constable and ineffectual by nature, he's pretty sensitive.

180

ANDY (deep disgust)
Joe Haller couldn't find his own ass if someone
rammed it full of radium and gave him a Geiger
counter.

PETE SYLVESTER (comes over)
Could be I know a fella who's still PO'd over
getting fined two hundred bucks for that little
fender bender out on the Ridge Road last year.

ANDY
Could be *I* know a fat old fella who ought to take
care of his mouth before someone comes along and
turns it inside out. I pay Joe Haller's salary to keep
the people in this town safe, and he ain't doing it.

140 INT.   BILLY McCLAREN, AT THE BAR   140

He's looking toward the table where the Fairton group sits.

BILLY (mildly)
Last town report said you was in arrears your
taxes, Andy. Guess you must have paid up, huh?

141 INT.   THE FAIRTON TABLE   141
ANDY
What are you, trying to be smart?

OWEN KNOPFLER comes over.

OWEN
You guys turn down the thermostat or I'm gonna
turn you all out. Now who's drinking?

ANDY (sulks)
Bring me a Schlitz.

142 EXT.   A TREE, WITH BRADY'S SMILE-KITE STUCK IN IT   DUSK   142

SOUND of panting.

MARTY comes into the frame, pulling himself up by the arms. His
arms are very strong, although his legs trail limply behind him (like
the tail of a kite). He sits on a branch, untangles the kite and the
string, and looks down.

MARTY (calls)
Here it comes!

143 EXT.   THE FOOT OF THE TREE, WITH BRADY   143
BRADY
Drop it!

As the kite flutteres down, JANE comes biking up.

181

                              JANE
              Marty Coslaw, you get down out of that tree!

144 EXT.   MARTY, IN THE TREE   144

     He descends, then hangs from the lowest branch.

                              MARTY
              Push the Bullet over, Jane, okay?

145 EXT.   MARTY AND JANE   145

                    JANE (makes no immediate move to do so)
              Supper was an hour ago, Dumbo.

                    MARTY (hanging)
              Oh, Jeez! I forgot! Is she mad?

                              JANE
              They *both* are. At me, for not getting you sooner. I
              ought to let you fall.

     But she pushes the chair over and MARTY drops into it. He pushes
     the starter and the Silver Bullet fires up.

146 EXT.   BRADY, FLYING HIS KITE ON THE COMMON   DUSK   146

                    MARTY (voice)
              Hey, Brady! You coming?

                    BRADY (looking into the sky)
              In a while!

     BRADY could give a shit if MARTY'S in trouble. He just waves
     vaguely. He's into the kite-flying experience, as the folks in Marin
     County might say.

147 EXT.   MARTY AND JANE   147

     He's looking toward the common, frowning and uncertain.

                              JANE
              Come *on*, Marty.

     She starts biking away. Marty starts after her, pauses, and looks at:

148 EXT.   BRADY, ON THE COMMON   DUSK   148

     CAMERA PANS SLOWLY UP to the yellow smile-kite in the bluish-
     purple sky.

149 INT.   OWEN'S PUB   LATE DUSK   149

     The former patrons are still here, with the exceptions of LOWE,
     BILLY McCLAREN, and BOBBY ROBERTSON. Many others have
     appeared; this is Happy Hour. Among them we see MR. ASPINALL,

                              182

the principal, and PELTZER, the druggist. A barmaid, NORMA, circulates with drinks and beers.

Speaking of beer, ANDY FAIRTON has gotten through a fair amount of Schlitz. It hasn't mellowed him, however; he is more belligerent than ever.

> ANDY (holding forth)
> This whole investigation has been as efficient as a
> Polish fire drill! It—

> PETE (bravely)
> I've heard enough out of you, Andy. If you don't
> shut your mouth, I'm going to shut it for you.

150 INT.   THE DOOR OF OWEN'S PLACE   150

It opens and a man in a business suit—HERB KINCAID—comes in. He is carrying a briefcase and he looks worried.

151 INT.   THE GROUP AT THE FAIRTON TABLE   151

> ANDY (astounded)
> *Wha-aat* did you say?

152 INT.   THE BAR, WITH OWEN KNOPFLER   152

> OWEN
> Jesus wept.

He reaches under the bar and comes out with a baseball bat. Burned into the side of the bat, so it reads vertically toward the handle, is the word *peacemaker*. ALFIE hurries around the bar with it.

153 INT.   THE FAIRTON GROUP   153

PETE is standing in front of ANDY, fists balled up, fat face trembling with determination.

> PETE
> You heard what I said, motormouth.

ANDY gets up, infuriated. There's apparently going to be a brawl. Behind them, HERB KINCAID has approached the table. HERB hasn't even noticed what's going on; he's got problems of his own.

154 INT.   HERB KINCAID   154

He clears his throat. This is a mild, timid man—he doesn't like to speak in public, particularly not in a bar, but the imperatives of the situation demand it right now.

> HERB (quite loudly)
> *Has anyone in here seen my son Brady?*

155   INT.   THE PUB, A NEW ANGLE   155

Everyone looks at HERB. Conversation stops. ANDY and PETE
freeze with their fists balled up, like little kids playing statues tag.
OWEN is caught a little distance from ANDY and PETE, with the
peacemaker still in his hands.

156   EXT.   THE TOWN COMMON, LONG   156

Now it is almost completely dark, and a large reddish summer moon
is rising over the horizon.

SOUND: A LONG, WAVERING WOLF HOWL . . . *LOUD.*

157   INT.   OWEN'S PUB   157

All conversation has stopped. All have turned toward the door and
the windows; all hear the HOWL. Deep fright overlies each face.

NORMA drops her tray. Glasses and bottles shatter.

158   INT.   THE MAIN CORRIDOR OF THE TOWN HALL   158

JOE HALLER comes out of the constable's office in a hurry, letting
the door bang the wall. He's buckling on his gun belt.

159   EXT.   THE BANDSTAND   159

BRADY'S kite, torn in a couple of places, flutters on the steps
leading up to the bandstand. The yellow smile face grins eerily in the
darkness. It is streaked with blood.

160   INT.   OWEN'S PUB   160
                           HERB
            Brady!

He breaks for the door. ANDY FAIRTON grabs him.

                           HERB
            Get out of my way!

He pushes ANDY aside. HERB is out the door, chased by PETE and
several of the others.

161   EXT.   THE BANDSTAND   NIGHT   161
                    JOE HALLER (low voice)
            Hail Mary, full of grace, the Lord is with thee.
            Blessed art thou among women . . .

He comes out of the shadows, his drawn gun dangling by his side.
This man has had an extremely bad shock. The legs of his uniform
pants are splashed with blood. He makes it down two steps and
then sits heavily by the remains of BRADY'S smiling, bloody kite. He
looks straight ahead. He looks at nothing.

> HALLER (low)
> ...and blessed is the fruit of Thy womb, Jesus.
> Holy Mary, Mother of God, pray for us sinners now
> ...now...

He looks at the kite, then looks away. He puts a hand over his face and starts to cry.

162 EXT.   THE COMMON, LOOKING BACK TOWARD MAIN STREET   162
NIGHT

A number of men—not all that were in Alfie's but quite a few of them—are running toward the bandstand. HERB KINCAID is in the lead, screaming his son's name over and over.

SOUND: A LONG HOWL, now at some distance.

163 EXT.   THE BANDSTAND, WITH HALLER AND KINCAID   163

As HERB KINCAID approaches.

> HALLER
> Stay off the bandstand, Herb.

> HERB
> It is my boy? Is it Brady?

> HALLER
> Don't go up—

> HERB (lunges past him)
> Brady! Brady!

Disappears into the dark. HALLER looks down at his lap.

> HERB
> Br—(CUTS OFF)

The other men arrive, PETE in the lead. HALLER doesn't look up.

> PETE
> Joe, is it—

> HALLER (not looking up)
> Shhh.

> PETE
> Is it the Kincaid b—

> HALLER (not looking up)
> Shhh, I said.

The men look uneasily at HALLER, at each other. ANDY FAIRTON shoves forward.

> ANDY
> What the fuck is going on h—

SOUND: HERB SCREAMS. A pause. HERB screams again. The men flinch back. HALLER doesn't look up. Now, from the darkness on the bandstand, HERB begins to LAUGH. The men shrink back further, looking more uneasy than ever.

> HERB (voice; laughing)
> We'll bury his *shoes*.

Now HALLER gets up and joins the other men.

> HERB (voice; laughing)
> That's what we'll have to do; we'll bury his *shoes*.
> Maybe in a couple of Roi-Tan cigar boxes.

164 EXT.   THE BANDSTAND, MEN'S POV NIGHT   164

HERB KINCAID appears. He is laughing. He is smeared with his son's blood. In each hand he holds one of his son's shoes.

> HERB
> We'll bury his *shoes* because his *feet* are still in them
> and they're the only part of him that makes sense
> anymore.

HERB laughs harder.

> HERB
> It's gonna be the cheapest funeral this town ever
> saw!

HERB SCREAMS LAUGHTER. THE CAMERA DOLLIES IN TO CLOSE ON BRADY'S KITE.

165 EXT.   THE MOON, CU   165

SOUND: HERB SCREAMING.

DISSOLVE TO:

166 EXT.   HOLY FAMILY CHURCH DAY   166

SOUND: An organ is playing that sweet old hymn, "Bringing in the Sheaves."

There are lots of cars parked in front of the church, but there's a space left just big enough for UNCLE AL'S MG. MARTY'S Silver Bullet is strapped to the back.

> JANE (v-o)
> My mother and father—my mother in particular—
> did not much care for Uncle Al . . .

167 INT.   HOLY FAMILY CHURCH DAY   167

MARTY'S chair is at the back of the church. Most of the mourners are crying. MRS. BOWIE is playing the organ. BRADY'S coffin is on a bier at the front—closed of course. There are lots of flowers.

JANE (v-o continues)
...but when it came to such unpleasant duties as
taking Marty to the funeral of his best friend...

168 INT.   UNCLE AL, MARTY, TAMMY, AND MRS. STURMFULLER,   168
IN A PEW

As we look at them, from left to right: UNCLE AL, MARTY,
TAMMY, MRS. STURMFULLER.

UNCLE AL unobtrusively takes a small silver flask from his hip
pocket. Engraved on it in Old English letters is the word *rotgut*. He
spins the cap and takes a quick knock. He pauses and glances at
MARTY, who looks deeply stunned.

JANE (v-o continues)
...they didn't at all mind drafting him. As to the
sort of comfort Uncle Al may have been able to
offer him...

UNCLE AL hands the flask to MARTY. MARTY looks at him
questioningly for a moment, and then drinks. MARTY looks at
TAMMY, who looks frankly terrible. Her mother is looking away.
MARTY nudges her. She looks around at him. He offers her the
flask. Her eyes widen.

JANE (v-o continues)
...I now believe that was best kept between the
two of them...

After a brief moment's consideration, TAMMY takes the flask and
has a deep swallow. She hands the flask back to MARTY, who hands
it quickly back to UNCLE AL as TAMMY coughs. Her mother looks
at her... then at MARTY and UNCLE AL. UNCLE AL smiles
sympathetically, hiding the flask with one hand, as if to say, "Isn't it
a terrible thing?" MRS. STURMFULLER looks distractedly back
toward the service.

JANE (v-o concludes)
...or among the three of them.

UNCLE AL pockets the flask just as the organ stops playing.

169 INT.   THE PODIUM, WITH FATHER LOWE   169

LOWE
Mr. and Mrs. Kincaid have asked that there be no
mass said here this afternoon. There will be a
requiem mass for Brady Kincaid this Sunday. They
did ask me to say a word of comfort to you, if I
could.

He looks out at them.

170 INT. THE CONGREGATION   170

They look back at LOWE, hoping for some help in understanding this awful thing.

171 INT. LOWE, ABOVE THE COFFIN   171

LOWE

If there is any word of comfort I can give you, it's
just this: the face of the beast always becomes
known; the time of the beast always passes.

He is struggling with this, trying dreadfully hard.

LOWE

If there are times when we feel alone and afraid,
only small creatures in the dark, then these are the
times when we must turn to one another for our
comfort and our hope. To our neighbors. To our
community. To our love for each other. I alone
cannot ease the pain for Herb and Naomi Kincaid,
nor can I ease your pain, nor you ease mine. But if
I believe anything it's this: we can comfort each
other. We can heal each other. We can go on
together.

172 INT. THE CONGREGATION, WITH MARTY AND TAMMY   172

The kids are crying. MARTY puts an arm around TAMMY and she
puts her head on his shoulder.

173 INT. FATHER LOWE   173

LOWE

The Bible tells us not to fear the terror that creepeth
by night or that which flieth by noonday, and yet
we do . . . we do. Because there is much we don't
know, and we feel very small. *But we must not be
alone.* We must not *allow* ourselves to be alone, for
there is the wide gate to the hell of terror. Turn to
each other. Join hands in your sorrow and try to
remember that the face of the beast always becomes
known. (Pause) The time of the beast always
passes. (Pause) Let us pray.

174 EXT. THE MOURNERS, WITH MARTY   174

MARTY and TAMMY look at each other miserably. TAMMY begins
to cry—for her father as much as for BRADY, one would think—and
she and MARTY embrace.

175 EXT. UNCLE AL, CU   175

He looks at the kids with deep sympathy and deep love.

188

176 EXT.   A COUNTRY ROAD   AFTERNOON   176

UNCLE AL'S sports car passes THE CAMERA. He's taking MARTY home.

177 INT.   THE CAR, WITH MARTY AND UNCLE AL   177

                         UNCLE AL
You all right, Marty?

                         MARTY
Yeah.

                         UNCLE AL
There's a saying—so-and-so was better than a poke in the eye with a sharp stick. You ever hear that one?

                         MARTY
No.

                         UNCLE AL
Well, I'm not sure *that* was. Christ! They better get the guy.

                         MARTY
Uncle Al, what if it's not a *guy*?

                         UNCLE AL
Huh?

                         MARTY
What if it's some kind of monster?

                         UNCLE AL (laughs)
Jesus, Marty! Come off it!

178 EXT.   UNCLE AL'S CAR, ON MAIN STREET   178

It cruises past Owen's Pub. There are cars parked out front, but there are also lots of pickup trucks.

179 INT.   THE CAR, WITH MARTY AND UNCLE AL   179

                         MARTY
What's going on at Owen's, Uncle Al?

                         UNCLE AL
A bunch of men getting ready to pretend they're Clint Eastwood. . . . Marty, didn't anybody ever tell you that the only monsters are in comic books and drive-in movies?

180 EXT.   THE COSLAW HOUSE   LATE AFTERNOON   180

UNCLE AL'S car turns in and parks.

189

181 INT.   THE CAR, WITH MARTY AND UNCLE AL   181

                         MARTY
          Tammy said she'd been hearing noises in that
          greenhouse. Growling noises, like a big animal. Her
          father was killed *that night*.

UNCLE AL looks at him doubtfully for a moment, as if almost
believing. Then shakes his head.

                       UNCLE AL
          Marty, you have to get this idea out of your head.
          Psychotics are more active when the moon is full,
          and this guy is a psycho. He's going to turn out to
          be as human as you or me. (Pause) In a manner of
          speaking. Now let's get you inside.

He opens his door and gets out.

182 INT.   MARTY, CLOSER   182

He would like to believe UNCLE AL . . . but he doesn't.

183 INT.   OWEN'S PUB   LATE AFTERNOON   183

                       ANDY FAIRTON
          Okay, you all know what group you're in and what
          area you'll be covering, right?

                     PORTER ZINNEMAN
          Damn straight!

                     ELMER ZINNEMAN
          Shut up, Porter.

The men are all dressed in hunting clothes—red-and-black-checked
shirts, orange caps, etc. They all have guns. Among their number
are a few women as well, looking tough and determined. We see
almost everyone we've met up to this point. LOWE is there, looking
deeply troubled.

ANDY FAIRTON is standing on the bar. These are his vigilantes; he
has organized them. ANDY radiates male macho football-coach
confidence. He's mesmerized the crowd; they really believe they are
going to go out and Shoot One for the Gipper.

                         ANDY
          Groups one through four are in the woods north of
          the Sturmfuller place. Five and six west of Carson
          Creek.

The door at the back opens; HALLER and PETE come in. JOE
HALLER is in extremely bad shape. He hasn't come back much from
the murder of BRADY. I believe he is having some sort of spiritual
crisis, and while it is not our purpose to explore what it might be—

this is, after all, a horror movie and not a John Cassavetes film—we can see that it has seriously weakened his authority.

                    ANDY (continuing)
          Moonrise at 8:52 P.M.

Some nervous laughter greets this. Meanwhile, HALLER and PETE are working their way to the front, where they end up next to a grim-faced HERB KINCAID.

                    ANDY (continuing)
          If he comes out to stroll in the moonlight tonight,
          we're going to get the sorry sucker.

184 INT.   THE VIGILANTES, WITH ELMER AND PORTER   184

                    PORTER (happily)
          Damn straight!

                    ELMER
          Shut up, Porter.

185 INT.   ANDY FAIRTON   185

                    ANDY
          Just remember, it's the psycho we want, not each
          other. So look before you—

186 INT.   THE CROWD, FEATURING HALLER   186

                    HALLER
          I want all of you folks to go home!

A disgruntled murmur meets this. HALLER moves forward a bit, and turns to face them.

                    HALLER
          I can't remember deputizing a single one of you!

187 INT.   ANDY FAIRTON   187

                    ANDY
          That's right, Joe—the only deputy you got is that
          fat shitbag beside you, and neither of you has done
          a damn thing about solving this case.

There is a mutter of agreement.

188 INT.   A SLIGHTLY WIDER SHOT, FEATURING ANDY AND   188
HALLER

ANDY hops off the bar to face HALLER directly. In the b.g. we see HERB KINCAID (KINCAID, by the way, should be wearing a black armband—he's come directly from his son's funeral).

191

HALLER (without much force)
We'll catch him.

ANDY
You couldn't catch a cold.

HALLER looks at him for a moment, then turns to look at the crowd. They look rather like a lynch mob; on their faces we see an uneasy mix of shame and eager determination. HALLER speaks with a kind of haggard, fading desperation.

HALLER
The law has a name for what you men are planning. It's private justice, and private justice is about a step and a half away from lynch mobs and hang ropes. I'm no J. Edgar Hoover, but I am the law in Tarker's Mills, *and I want you men to go home.*

They shuffle their feet uneasily; many look down. He is getting to them.

ANDY
Don't let this guy scare you! What's *he* done since this thing started but hang his face out?

It's not working. Many of the men look disgusted with both ANDY and themselves.

ANDY (louder)
He ain't got so much as a *fingerprint!*

OWEN KNOPFLER
Ah, shut up, Andy.

ANDY
Don't tell me to—

HERB KINCAID steps forward.

HERB
Yes. Correct. Shut up.

ANDY, surprised and bewildered, does. HERB turns and looks grimly at JOE HALLER, who can barely meet his gaze.

HERB (quietly)
I just came from my boy's funeral.

HALLER
Herb . . . I know how upset—how grief-stricken you must be . . . but—

HERB (quietly)
He was torn apart.

Utter silence in OWEN'S place now. The others are staring, rapt.

                    HALLER
Yes. Yes, but—

                    HERB (still quiet)
Upset, you say. Grief-stricken, you say. Constable
Haller, you don't know what those words *mean*. My
son was torn to pieces. To *pieces*!

HERB turns to the others in the pub. Tears stream down his face.

                    HERB
My son was torn to pieces!
                              (turning back to HALLER)
You come in here and talk to these men about
private justice. You dare to do that. Constable
Haller, why don't you go out to Harmony Hill and
dig up what's left of Brady and explain to him
about private justice. Would you want to do that?

HALLER makes no reply. He looks down at his feet.

                    HERB
No. I thought not.
                              (to the others)
You folks stay here if you want. I wouldn't ask
anyone to do anything which runs counter to his
conscience. As for me . . . I'm going out and hunt
up a little private justice.

ANDY FAIRTON has swelled up again. He grins poisonously at the
slumped HALLER. He pushes after HERB KINCAID. Other men
start to follow.

189 EXT.   OWEN'S PUB   189

Men are streaming out, getting into station wagons and pickup
trucks. Engines roar into life. They begin backing out even as more
men come out of the pub. We even hear some high-spirited yells;
they are on their way and their blood is up.

190 INT.   OWEN'S PUB   190

LESTER LOWE, looking more distressed than ever, pushes his way
through the men toward the door, and THE CAMERA FOLLOWS.
He grabs BILLY McCLAREN.

                    LOWE
Billy . . . Billy, this is a bad idea. Joe can . . .

                    BILLY (not looking at LOWE)
Joe's had his chance, Father. Leave me be.

He pushes outside. LOWE looks around wildly; his face says he
can't believe this is happening. He grabs PORTER ZINNEMAN,

                              193

then, as PORTER shoves by him, at a couple of others with increasing desperation.

HALLER makes his way to LOWE through the thinning crowd and draws him aside.

> HALLER
>
> Let them go.

> LOWE
>
> But—

> HALLER
>
> This is that spirit of community you were talking about. Grand, ain't it? Maybe they'll shoot a hitchhiker or something and Andy can mount the head and raffle it off. To benefit the Medcu van, of course.

HALLER laughs.

> LOWE
>
> But can't we do *anything*?

OWEN KNOPFLER hurries past them; he has a rifle over one shoulder in a sling. In his left hand he carries the peacemaker bat.

> HALLER
>
> Sure. We can pray to Christ that none of them get killed.

191 EXT.   OUTSIDE OWEN'S   191

More cars and trucks pull away. There's a big old Ford "woody" wagon still there, with ANDY FAIRTON standing impatiently by the driver's side door. BILLY McCLAREN and BOBBY ROBERTSON are with him, and a big, solid-looking woman named MAGGIE ANDREWS.

ALFIE comes out and crosses to the woody.

> ANDY
>
> Well, it's about frigging time! They'll have his hide tacked to somebody's barn door before we get out there!

They pile into the car, ANDY behind the wheel. He throws it into gear and backs out onto Main Street.

192 EXT.   MAIN STREET, A NEW ANGLE   192

We see a parade of cars and pickup trucks headed out of town.

193 INT.   FATHER LESTER LOWE   193

He's standing on the curb and watching them leave town in
procession, some honking their horns, others yelling cheerfully. The
expression on his thin face is dark and brooding.

194 EXT.   THE FULL MOON, CU NIGHT   194

195 EXT.   ELMER AND PORTER ZINNEMAN   NIGHT   195

ELMER is lying on his belly, stuck halfway under a barbed-wire
fence. The seat of his pants is badly snagged. The brothers are on
the verge of a wooded area. We can see ground mist creeping
around the bottoms of the trees.

                    ELMER
        Help me Porter, goddammit!

PORTER grabs ELMER'S right arm and pulls. There's a RIPPING
SOUND. ELMER screams.

                    ELMER
        Don't *pull* me! You want to rip the right cheek of
        my ass right off?

                    PORTER
        Well, Elmer, there are folks that'd say you've been
        half-assed most of your—

                    ELMER
        Are you going to unhook me or be a wise guy?

PORTER begins to pick the barbed wire out of ELMER'S pants.

196 EXT.   IN THE WOODS, WITH REV. O'BANION AND VIRGIL   196
CUTTS   NIGHT

O'BANION looks rather amusing in his hunting gear—like that
priest from *The Exorcist* on safari.

SOUND: A HOWL, FAIRLY LOUD.

                    VIRGIL
        Jesus, that was *close*. Uh, pardon me, Rev'runt.

                    O'BANION
        Come on. Be careful.

They move slowly ahead, O'BANION still a bit in the lead. THE
CAMERA FOLLOWS as the reverend pushes into some knee-high
brush.

SOUND: A RUSTY METALLIC CLANG, followed by a FLESHY
CHOMP.

O'BANION begins to scream and struggle.

> VIRGIL
> *Rev'runt!* What is it?

> O'BANION (screaming)
> My foot! My *fooot!*

VIRGIL lunges to him and looks down.

197 EXT.   O'BANION'S FOOT, VIRGIL'S POV   197

A medium-sized trap—something in which one might reasonably hope to catch a wildcat or a coydog, let us say—has its rusty teeth sunk deeply into the reverend's ankle.

198 EXT.   O'BANION AND VIRGIL   198

> O'BANION (SCREAMING)
> *Get it off me! Get it off me!*

> VIRGIL (flustered)
> Sure . . . okay . . .

He kneels down.

199 EXT.   VIRGIL   199

He muscles the trap open, a little at a time.

200 EXT.   O'BANION   200

Relaxing.

SOUND: THE WOLF HOWLING CLOSE.

201 EXT.   VIRGIL   201

Startled and unnerved by the HOWL, the trap slips out of his hands and snaps shut on O'BANION'S mangled ankle again.

202 EXT.   REVEREND O'BANION   202

He screams.

203 EXT.   THE MOON, CU   203

It slides behind a cloud.

SOUND: THE WOLF, HOWLING.

204 EXT.   ANDY FAIRTON'S GROUP   204

ANDY, BILLY McCLAREN, BOBBY ROBERTSON, OWEN KNOPFLER, and MAGGIE ANDREWS have been joined by two other men—MR. ASPINALL and EDGAR ROUNDS.

They have drawn close together, listening as the HOWL FADES. We can tell by their uneasy faces that some of the joy has gone out of the evening.

They are standing on one side of a ravine. The bottom is filled with a still ground mist. A few bushes poke out of it. There are woods on the far side.

> ANDY (pointing across)
> It came from over there.

> BOBBY ROBERTSON
> As far as I could tell, it could have come from *anywhere.*

> ANDY
> We'll spread out in a skirmish line. If the bastard tries to go around us, we'll hear him.

> BOBBY
> I dunno—

> MAGGIE
> I think Bobby Robertson here's making lemonade in his pants. That lemonade got ice cubes in it, Bobby?

ANDY FAIRTON and EDGAR ROUNDS laugh: ASPINALL and BILLY McCLAREN smile a little.

> OWEN (quietly)
> Let off him, Maggie. I'm scared, too.

> BOBBY (stoutly)
> I ain't scared! Let's go!

> ANDY
> Okay. Spread out on me. Five feet apart.

205　EXT.　　ANDY'S GROUP, FROM THE BOTTOM OF THE RAVINE　　　205

Reading from right to left: OWEN KNOPFLER (his gun is still over his shoulder; it is the peacemaker baseball bat he is holding), BOBBY ROBERTSON, ASPINALL, ANDY FAIRTON, BILLY McCLAREN, EDGAR ROUNDS and MAGGIE ANDREWS.

They come slowly down toward THE CAMERA, alert and ready for anything—at least, they *think* so.

206　EXT.　　ANDY'S GROUP, ANGLE SHOT　　　206

They reach the bottom of the ravine and begin to make their way across it. The mist is waist to chest deep. They push toward the other side. Now they are about halfway.

SOUND: A STEADY LOW GROWLING, CLOSE.

They all stop, scared.

> BILLY McCLAREN
> Where's it coming from? Other side?

> BOBBY
> No—it's *behind* us. I *told* you you couldn't trust—

> ASPINALL
> It isn't on *either* side.

> ANDY
> What are you—

ASPINALL is looking around, his eyes widening with fear.

> ASPINALL
> It's under the fog. *It's right in WITH us.*

The GROWLING STOPS. There's a beat of silence. Then:

SOUND: SNARLING . . . AND A RIPPING CHOMP as dinner is served.

SOUND: A SCREAM.

207 EXT.   EDGAR ROUNDS, CLOSE   207

He's the one screaming, and if he reminds us of O'BANION, that's okay, because ROUNDS has *also* been caught in a trap. He tries to run, stumbles, falls into the ground fog. He goes on screaming. We can see his back for a moment, and then it disappears.

SOUNDS OF CRUNCHING AND MUNCHING.

ROUNDS SHRIEKS. His hand and arm come up like the hand of a drowning man. Then it's gone. ROUNDS is gone.

208 EXT.   THE SKIRMISH LINE   208

They stand there, chest deep in mist, a conspicuous hole in the ranks where EDGAR was.

209 EXT.   BOBBY ROBERTSON, CU   209

> BOBBY (moaning)
> I can't move. Christ Jesus, I can't move!

210 EXT.   THE SKIRMISH LINE IN THE RAVINE, A NEW ANGLE   210

The GROWLING STARTS AGAIN. THE CAMERA PANS SLOWLY UP THE LINE. The mist swirls, hiding whatever's beneath.

211 EXT.   ASPINALL, CU   211

> ASPINALL (low)
> I think we better start backing up, Andy. Real slow.
> Real—

The LOW GROWL rises to a snarl. And from below the mist, snarling and bestial but understandable, mocking ASPINALL'S voice:

> WEREWOLF (voice)
> "Real slow! Real slow! Real slow!"

SOUND: CHOMP!

ASPINALL SHRIEKS and tries to run. He falls into the mist. There is another CHOMP. When he flounders up, half his face is gone.

> WEREWOLF (voice)
> "Real slow! Real slow!"

A hairy arm rises from the mist and yanks ASPINALL down.

212 EXT.   ANDY'S GROUP   212

They panic and break for it—MAGGIE, BILLY, and ANDY for one side, BOBBY and OWEN for the other.

213 EXT.   OWEN, WEREWOLF'S POV   213

THE CAMERA IS RUSHING THROUGH THE GROUND MIST—this is like being in an airplane that's skimming the top of a cloud.

> WEREWOLF (voice; laughing)
> "Real slow! Real slow! Real slow!"

214 EXT.   OWEN KNOPFLER   214

He's *hit*, as an unlucky swimmer might be hit by a shark. He whirls around, raising the peacemaker bat.

> OWEN
> Come on, then! You want to rock and roll with me?

215 EXT.   THE GROUND MIST, OWEN'S POV   215

For a moment there's nothing—and then the werewolf rises out of it, eyes glaring green, muzzle and pelt slimed with gore.

> WEREWOLF
> *"REEEEEL SLOW!"*

216 EXT.   MAGGIE AND ANDY   216

> MAGGIE (shrieking)
> Look at it! Holy God, Andy, *look at that thing*!

ANDY (groaning with fear)
I don't want to look at it.

He runs, while MAGGIE stares, mesmerized, at:

217 EXT.   OWEN AND THE WEREWOLF   217

The WEREWOLF closes in on OWEN, who belts it a good one with
the peacemaker. The WEREWOLF swipes at him. ALFIE ducks and
slams it again. The WEREWOLF roars with anger.

OWEN
Come on, come on! You want to do the bop? I'll
bop you, motherfucker! Come on!

The WEREWOLF dives under the ground mist.

Uncertain, OWEN begins to back up, holding the bat in his hands.
OWEN is jerked down into the mist. He SCREAMS. The peacemaker
rises out of the ground mist and comes down. *Bonk!* The
WEREWOLF roars in pain. CHOMPING SOUND. OWEN shrieks.

OWEN (voice)
Come on, you bastard!

The peacemaker rises out of the mist again. The hands holding it are
bloody. Blood runs down the bat. It descends. *Bonk!* The
WEREWOLF roars again. There is a GURGLING SCREAM from
OWEN . . . and then a curious SPLINTERING SOUND as the
WEREWOLF sinks its fangs into the bat.

218 EXT.   THE RAVINE   218

THE CAMERA MOVES ABOVE as the WEREWOLF moves below,
escaping down the draw.

Pause. SOUND, IN THE B.G.—low but slowly getting louder: a
congregation singing "Bringing in the Sheaves" to the
accompaniment of a pipe organ.

WEREWOLF (sing-songy voice)
Bringing in the sheaves . . . bringing in the sheaves
. . . we shall come rejoicing . . . bringing in the
sheaves. . . .

The WEREWOLF FADES OUT; human voices singing the same
hymn overwhelm it and we

DISSOLVE TO:

219 INT.   HOLY FAMILY CATHOLIC CHURCH, PULPIT POV   219
MORNING

It's an almost exact reprise of #167. Most of the mourners are crying;
MRS. BOWIE playing the organ; MARTY'S chair parked at the back.
We can see UNCLE AL, MARTY, TAMMY, and MRS.

STURMFULLER, exactly as they were at BRADY KINCAID'S funeral; in fact, this seems to be an instant replay of that event. One difference: we can't see BRADY'S coffin. It's below us. The hymn ends.

220 INT. FATHER LOWE, IN THE PULPIT   220

>LOWE
>Mr. and Mrs. Kincaid have asked that there be no
>mass said here this afternoon. They did ask me to
>say a word of comfort to you if I could.

221 INT. THE CONGREGATION, FEATURING HERB KINCAID   221

He sits in the first pew. In his grief he looks dead.

>HERB
>There is no comfort, Father. Only private justice.

222 INT. LOWE, AT THE PULPIT   222

He's thrown off his stride. Beginning to sweat. He's like an actor trying to remember his lines.

>LOWE
>Uh, if there's any word of comfort I can give you,
>it's just this: the face of the beast always becomes
>known; the time—

He looks down. His eyes widen in fear.

223 INT. THE COFFINS, LOWE'S POV   223

Yes, that's *coffins*—plural. Where BRADY'S coffin was formerly, there are now *six* caskets, smothered with flowers.

224 INT. LOWE, IN THE PULPIT   224

He is badly scared now; sweat is dripping off him.

>LOWE
>The time . . . the time of the beast always passes.
>There are answers . . . ways . . . ways to . . . to cope
>. . . if we turn to each other. . . .
>   HERB (bestial voice)
>Father—

LOWE looks toward:

225 INT. FIRST ROW PEW, WITH HERB KINCAID, LOWE'S POV   225

He's looking down at something in his hands. Now he looks up and we see his face has become bestial. His eyes are green. As we look at him, the transformation continues. He's turning into a werewolf.

HERB (snarling)
It tore out his heart.

And sure enough, HERB KINCAID holds BRADY'S dripping heart up in what were hands but which are now rapidly becoming paws.

226   INT.   LESTER LOWE, AT THE PULPIT   226

He staggers back, in terror.
                    LOWE (shrieks)
          No!

227   INT.   THE CONGREGATION, LOWE'S POV   227

MRS. BOWIE begins bringing in a few more sheaves on the church organ, and the congregation begins to sing.
                    CONGREGATION
          Sowing in the morning/sowing seeds of kindness/
          sowing in the noontide/and the dewy eve...

We pan their faces, stopping on JOE HALLER. Now something is happening to JOE'S face. It is bulging; changing. He looks up from his hymnal and his eyes glare green. The pupils are split. He grins, showing big teeth.

They are *all* changing. Among the things we see are:

PETE SYLVESTER, who is a church deacon, rushing down the aisle, changing, snarling. He grabs ANDY FAIRTON, and the two of them grapple in the aisle.

A YOUNG WOMAN with a baby in her arms turns back the blanket covering the baby's face and we see it's a wolfling; already the YOUNG WOMAN'S own hands are turning into claws.

TAMMY STURMFULLER changing; PELTZER the druggist changing; the ZINNEMAN BROTHERS changing.

At the organ, MRS. BOWIE is now a werewolf clad in tatters of a silk bombazine dress; she/it is still wearing a veiled hat on her head, and she is beating the *shit* out of the organ keys with her clawed hands. She sounds like Jerry Lee Lewis might after swallowing about a dozen bennies. And now the tune changes from the remnants of "Bringing in the Sheaves." It changes into the Rheingold jingle.

                    CONGREGATION (snarling chorus)
          My beer is Rheingold the *dry* beer...
          Think of Rheingold whenever you *buy* beer...

228   INT.   LOWE   228

FATHER LOWE goes stumbling backward, dropping his hymnal. The man is in an extremity of terror.

202

REV. LOWE
No! No! No!

229 INT.   THE CONGREGATION, LOWE'S POV   229

Some are tearing their hymnals apart and throwing them at each
other. One guy—BILLY McCLAREN, maybe—wings one of them
through a stained-glass window. Some of the werewolves—for they
are all werewolves now—fight or make love in the aisles. The rest
sway back and forth, grinning ferociously, singing.

CONGREGATION (snarling it out)
It's not *bitter*, not *sweet*, it's a real frosty *treat* . . .

230 INT.   LOWE   230

He looks toward:

231 INT.   THE MRS. BOWIE WEREWOLF, AT THE ORGAN   231

She grins ferociously up at him, playing the Rheingold jingle on the
pipe organ with her claws. Now blood begins to bubble up between
the keys.

MRS. STURMFULLER AND ALL
Won't you try, won't you buy . . .

232 INT.   THE ENTIRE CONGREGATION   232

The church is a wild shambles of lurching, fighting, singing
werewolves. It's like a New Year's Eve party in hell.

CONGREGATION (big finish)
. . . *Rheiiinngold beer!*

Suddenly a clawed hand bursts up through one of the coffins. And
ANDY FAIRTON, who now looks as wolflike as any of them, bites
the hand's claw off.

233 INT.   REV. LOWE, ON THE PODIUM   233

He's seen all he can stand. He whirls for the back, where there is a
small door. He pulls it open . . . and a BRADY KINCAID werewolf,
half torn apart but still somehow alive (a zombie werewolf, if you
can dig it—George Romero would like it, I think) leaps out and
seizes LOWE.

BRADY buries his muzzle in LOWE'S NECK.

234 INT.   LESTER LOWE, ECU   234

He sits up into THE CAMERA and SCREAMS. Sweat is running
down his face. He stares at us for a moment, his eyes buggy and
crazed . . . and then he closes them. There is an expression of huge
relief on his face as he does so.

LOWE (praying)
Let it end, dear Lord. Let it end. Please let it end.

235 EXT.   MAIN STREET   DAY   235

An old sedan cruises slowly down the street. ANNE and TAMMY
STURMFULLER are in the front seat. It's piled high with possessions
and is towing a jackleg trailer with more stuff in it.

236 EXT.   HALLER AND PETE   236

HALLER (indifferently)
Anne Sturmfuller and her little girl.

PETE
Yeah . . . but what are they doing?

HALLER
Putting on my Sherlock Holmes deerstalker cap, I
deduce that they are leaving.

237 EXT.   THE STURMFULLER CAR, THE COPS' POV   DAY   237

They are headed out of town all right, but the thing which perhaps
strikes us the most forcibly is how *empty* this place is now. Main
Street looks like a ghost town.

238 EXT.   JOE HALLER AND PETE SYLVESTER, ON THE SIDEWALK   238

HALLER
She's not the only one. Lot of people leaving town.
And I guess if we want a beer, we'll have to drink
it at home.

He nods toward:

239 EXT.   OWEN'S PUB LONG (PETE AND HALLER'S POV)   239

A CLOSED sign hangs in the door; above it is a big black wreath.

240 EXT.   HALLER AND PETE   240

PETE
Joe, what's wrong with you? I ain't *never* seen you
like this.

HALLER (thoughtful)
I lost my guts.

PETE (startled)
Bullshit!

HALLER
It was the Kincaid boy. I looked at him . . . and I felt
it happen. It was no big deal. No worse than

204

pissing down your own leg. You ever do that?
Maybe when you were real scared?

PETE, distressed, does not respond.

> HALLER
> One minute I had me some guts—as much as the
> next man, anyhow—and then, poof. Gone.

PETE'S looking at him in a kind of terror.

> PETE
> Joe . . . you are going to feel better than this. This . . .
> this feeling of yours . . . it's gonna pass.

> JOE
> Is it?

He walks away, back toward the Municipal Building (the sign out
front reminds folks to SUPPORT THE MEDCU VAN!) while PETE looks
after him, very deeply troubled.

241   EXT.   A FAIRGROUND   DAY   241

It's deserted. Rides stand still. The midway is deserted.

THE CAMERA PANS slowly to a sign which reads TARKER'S MILLS
FAIRGROUNDS GALA FAIR OCTOBER 1 FIREWORKS AT DUSK 10¢ ON EVERY
DOLLAR GOES TO THE MEDCU VAN FUND!

A cheerful enough sign, except for the strip of paper glued
diagonally across it: FIREWORKS CANCELED.

> MARTY (voice)
> It's not *fair*.

242   INT.   THE COSLAW FAMILY STATION WAGON   DAY   242

It is parked across the road from the sign.

> JANE (voice)
> Look out, world! Marty the Great didn't get
> something he wanted!

They are distributed just as they were when they arrived at this
same fairgrounds earlier. All of them have ice cream cones; they are
coming home from a family outing.

> NAN COSLAW
> Stop it, Jane.

> JANE
> Well, I don't see why everybody just about breaks
> down and *cries* whenever he—

> BOB
> Stop it, your mother said.

They've just paused for a quick look at the sign; now BOB pulls out onto the road again and heads toward home.

243   INT.   MARTY AND JANE IN THE BACKSEAT   243

JANE sticks her tongue out at him. MARTY looks away.

244   EXT.   ANGLE ON THE COSLAW GARAGE   DAY   244

UNCLE AL'S sports car is parked in the driveway. We hear the CLANG of a wrench on the cement inside.

245   INT.   THE GARAGE   DAY   245

UNCLE AL and MARTY are working on the engine of the Silver Bullet. UNCLE AL has a six-pack of beer that he's working through. He and MARTY sit on the floor. As they talk, UNCLE AL unscrews the last bolt holding the Bullet's carburetor and pulls it off.

> MARTY
> It isn't enough that the monster killed all those people—that he killed *Brady*. Now he's got them to cancel the fair.

> UNCLE AL
> And the fireworks. Hand me that box, Marty.

MARTY hands him a medium-sized carton with the words *Speed Shop* printed on it.

> MARTY
> Yeah, okay, the fireworks. Jane thinks that's all I'm mad about, but it's not. Them doing that is just a
> . . . a . . .

> UNCLE AL
> It's just an outward symbol of everything that's inwardly wrong in this town. Not bad, huh? I read Sherwood Anderson in college. I can jive that shit all day.

> MARTY
> Well . . . I like it that you always know how to say things, Uncle Al.

> UNCLE AL
> I'll give you the telephone numbers of my ex-wives, dear boy—they'll be interested to hear that.

> MARTY
> Don't call me dear boy.

> UNCLE AL
> But you are, you know—you *are* my dear boy.

He gives MARTY a kiss and smiles at him. MARTY smiles back.

UNCLE AL
Look at this.

He pulls out a brand-new carburetor—it's a chrome-plated four-barrel.

UNCLE AL (gleeful)
This is gonna turn your wheelchair into a fucking F-14, Marty—

He looks around quickly, guiltily.

UNCLE AL
Your mom's not around, is she?

MARTY
She and dad are out back lighting the barbecue. Jane's walking around like she's King Shit of Turd Mountain. Like always.

UNCLE AL
Uh-huh. Only in her case I guess it would be *Queen* Shit of Turd Mountain. Hand me that adjustable.

MARTY does. UNCLE AL slides the carb onto the gasket and starts attaching bolts.

UNCLE AL
The guy killed your best friend, drove your girl out of town, and stole the second-best holiday in the year. Have I got it right?

MARTY (glum)
You got it right, Uncle Al.

UNCLE AL
Yeah, Winesburg, Ohio, was never like *that* . . . but I got something that just might cheer you up.

MARTY
What?

UNCLE AL
Wait, dear boy. Just wait. Hand me those pliers.

246   EXT.   UNCLE AL, AT THE SIDE OF THE COSLAW HOUSE   DAY   246

He peeks into the backyard.

247   EXT.   THE BACK YARD, UNCLE AL'S POV   247

BOB and NAN are fussing over the barbecue. JANE is hitting a badminton birdie.

248   EXT.   THE ROAD IN FRONT OF COSLAWS', WITH MARTY   248

MARTY is sitting in the Silver Bullet.

UNCLE AL comes hurrying back from his look-see.

UNCLE AL
All is cool, Marty-boy. Go for it.

MARTY pushes the starter. The engine starts at once, but the tone is entirely different. Before, MARTY'S wheelchair was a poppety-popping pussycat. Now the engine rumbles like a hood's street rod idling at a traffic light.

MARTY looks startled.

UNCLE AL (grinning)
Gun it.

MARTY guns it. The engine *roars*.

UNCLE AL
Jesus! Not too much!

MARTY (awed)
Wow.

UNCLE AL
You got a pilot's license, Marty?

MARTY
Do I need one?

UNCLE AL
We're gonna find out. Take it down the road a
ways and back. Be careful.

MARTY puts the Bullet in gear and pulls away.

249 EXT.   MARTY, IN THE SILVER BULLET   249

CAMERA TRACKS HIM up the road. He goes slowly at first, but he lets it out a little after a while. He's really moving along—thirty, maybe forty miles an hour. The wind blows the hair off his forehead. He begins to grin. He's enjoying this.

250 EXT.   UNCLE AL, WATCHING   250

He drinks some beer. He's grinning, happy for MARTY.

251 EXT.   MARTY, IN THE SILVER BULLET   251

He slows down, turns, stops. He revs the engine. VROOM!
VRROOM!

252 EXT.   THE SILVER BULLET'S MOTOR, CU   252

A lot of changes back here. It looks almost like a motorcycle engine now. That chromed-silver carb predominates.

SOUND: *VAROOOOOOOM!*

253 EXT.   MARTY, CU   253

Grinning. Looking at:

254 EXT.   THE COSLAW HOUSE, MARTY'S POV   254

It's about a quarter of a mile away.

255 EXT.   MARTY, IN THE SILVER BULLET   255

He winds the engine up and pops the clutch. The Silver Bullet
doesn't so much accelerate as blast off. It tilts back on its wheels.
MARTY swivels into a position like that of an astronaut on lift-off.
The Silver Bullet looks like a motorcycle popping a wheelie. MARTY
has a great big grin on his face.

256 EXT.   THE SILVER BULLET, MEDIUM-LONG   256

Roaring down the highway at fifty or better, blue smoke jetting from
the exhaust. MARTY is plastered back in the seat with the footrest
pointing up at an angle. He's laughing like a lunatic.

257 EXT.   UNCLE AL, PEEKING THROUGH HIS FINGERS   257

UNCLE AL (to himself)
The kid's dead meat. What have I done?
(shouts)
Put a rock in it, Marty!

258 EXT.   MARTY IN THE BULLET   258

He uses the hand brakes. SOUND of braking and squealing rubber.

259 EXT.   MARTY AND UNCLE AL   259

The Silver Bullet comes to a screeching, sluing stop near UNCLE AL.
Blue smoke drifts up from the wheels. MARTY guns the engine once
and then lets it idle.

UNCLE AL
You gave me a heart attack, Marty. I'm dying. I
hope you're happy, because you are looking at a
dying man.

MARTY
It really goes fast. Thanks, Uncle Al.

UNCLE AL
It goes fast, all right—and if your mother finds out
just *how* fast, Marty, I will have a new job. Singing
soprano with the Vienna Boys' Choir.

MARTY
I don't get you.

209

UNCLE AL
I know you don't. But I want this to be our secret.
You get that, don't you?

MARTY
Sure.

UNCLE AL
Good.

260   EXT.   THE NIGHT SKY, WITH THE MOON   260

The last bit of daylight is just filtering away.

261   EXT.   THE COSLAW BACKYARD   261

The barbecue is over. BOB and JANE are putting lawn chairs on the
back porch. MARTY, NAN, and UNCLE AL are all in the f.g.

UNCLE AL
I've got to go, Nan—I had a wonderful time.

He kisses her cheek affectionately, and she smiles at him.

NAN
So have I, actually . . . I wish it could always be like
this.

UNCLE AL
See me around to my car, Marty, and make sure I
stay out of trouble at least that long.

MARTY
Okay.

He and UNCLE AL go around to the driveway. NAN looks at them
with troubled love.

262   EXT.   THE COSLAW DRIVEWAY, WITH MARTY AND UNCLE AL   262

UNCLE AL
Now I said I had something for you, as I believe
you will recall.

MARTY
Yeah! What is it?

AL unlocks the trunk of his car and brings out a paper shopping
bag. He places the bag in MARTY'S lap. MARTY opens the bag, but
it's really too dark to see inside. He reaches in and brings out a
handful of assorted fireworks—crackers, Roman candles, twizzers,
smoke bombs, etc.

An expression of sublime delight fills MARTY'S face as he
inventories these goodies.

> UNCLE AL
> You're gonna have the Fourth of July in October,
> Marty. Just don't blow your head off. (Pause) And
> remember that it isn't just the fireworks. It's
> because no crazy shithead should be able to stop
> the good guys, if you can dig that.

> MARTY (respectfully)
> I can dig it—thank you, Uncle Al! Thank you!

> UNCLE AL
> Stay near the house, for Christ's sake—someone's
> killing people. I have to be out of my mind to be
> doing this, you know.

> MARTY
> Yeah, I know. It's great!

> UNCLE AL
> One of the reasons I love you, Marty, is that you're
> almost as crazy as I am. Please don't set off
> anything that goes bang tonight, okay? Just bright
> colors. Can you tell the difference?

> MARTY
> Yeah . . . sure.

> UNCLE AL
> Save this one for last.

He brings out a short rocket with stubby vanes on the end. A fat
fuse sticks out behind the head.

> MARTY
> What is it?

> UNCLE AL
> A tracer. You'll like it.

> MARTY
> Thanks a *million*, Uncle Al!

> UNCLE AL
> You're welcome a million, Marty. Stick 'em in the
> bushes for now.

MARTY motors over to the side of the garage, where there's a line of
bushes, and conceals the bag in them. UNCLE AL gets in his car and
starts it up. MARTY comes back.

> UNCLE AL (grinning)
> Have a good time, dear boy. And watch out for the
> werewolves!

He leaves. Marty sits in his wheelchair, waving.

263 EXT.   THE REAR OF THE COSLAW HOUSE   NIGHT   263

There's a downspout outside one of the upstairs windows. Now the window goes up and MARTY leans out. He grasps the downspout and begins working his way down. This should not be too hard for us to believe; we've already seen how strong MARTY'S arms are.

His legs dangle limply, but he's doing just fine. When he reaches the bottom of the drainpipe, they simply crumple under him and he uses his arms to pull himself over to the back porch.

MARTY hoists himself over the porch rail. Here, under a tarp, is the Silver Bullet. MARTY pushes the tarp aside and gets in. He uses his hands on the wheels to get over to the porch ramp and rolls silently down it. At the bottom he looks up at:

264 EXT.   AN UPSTAIRS WINDOW, MARTY'S POV   NIGHT   264

Still a light on up there.

265 EXT.   MARTY, IN THE BULLET   265

MARTY (whispers)
Shit!

Thinks a bit, then starts to hand-roll the bullet toward:

266 EXT.   THE PATH BETWEEN THE HOUSE AND THE GARAGE   266

MARTY comes slowly up the path. We hear soft grunts of exertion; he's still hand-turning the wheels for the sake of silence, and it's hard work. He stops at the line of bushes and gets the bag of fireworks. He puts it on his lap and starts moving again.

267 EXT.   THE COSLAW DRIVEWAY, FROM THE ROAD   267

The driveway has a slight downslant, and MARTY coasts easily out to the road. He turns right and begins to roll slowly along the verge of the highway, still using his hands. We can see that the light is still on upstairs. MARTY turns back once to verify this himself, then keeps on going. He's not going to be deprived of his treat.

268 EXT.   MARTY   268

He decides he's far enough away to be safe. He pushes the starter button. The engine cranks, coughs, and cranks some more, MARTY frowns, and pulls out a wire—a rudimentary choke, I suppose. He pushes the starter button again. It cranks, but doesn't start.

MARTY pushes in the wire, looking concerned now, and tries again. This time, after the engine has cranked over a few times, it starts.

MARTY (softly)
All right!

He puts it in gear and starts off.

269 EXT.   THE ROAD, WITH MARTY, EXTREMELY LONG   269

What we see is a tiny boy in a tiny wheelchair moving along a dark, empty ribbon of road under a vast dome of stars.

DISTANT SOUND: The Bullet's engine.

270 EXT.   A ROADSIDE TURNOUT   NIGHT   270

SOUND: Fast-rushing water.

The turnout is packed dirt. There's a grove of trees with picnic tables spotted among them at the back. The sign in the extreme f.g. reads ROADSIDE REST AREA at the top; AUGER FALLS in the middle; TOWNSHIP OF TARKER'S MILLS at the bottom.

SOUND: The Silver Bullet approaching.

MARTY turns in and rolls to the back of the rest area. He stops by one of the picnic tables and dumps the bag of fireworks out onto the picnic table and takes his time selecting the first—he's like a wine fancier with a whole cellar of rare bottles to choose from. At last he chooses a twizzer. He takes matches from the pocket of his pajama top and lights the fuse.

When it starts to fizz, MARTY tosses it high into the air.

> MARTY (soft)
> Here's one for the good guys!

271 EXT.   THE TWIZZER   271

It flies in an arc over the drop.

272 EXT.   THE TWIZZER, FROM THE BOTTOM OF THE CUT   272

THE CAMERA TRACKS ITS FALL onto some rocks at the edge of the waterfall's catch pool.

SOUND: Growling.

273 EXT.   THE CREEK, WITH THE WEREWOLF   273

It has been drinking from the creek. It looks more than half human now—we would be able to recognize it for sure, but its face is in shadow.

It turns from the creek and gets up on its hind legs.

274 EXT.   THE TWIZZER, ON THE ROCKS   274

It's guttering out. A hand-paw touches it and draws back quickly.

SOUND: Hurt, angry growl.

275 EXT.   MARTY, IN THE REST AREA   275

He's getting ready to light one of the fountains. He pauses and looks toward the cut. He's heard something—but the waterfall muffles it. He lights the fountain's fuse, sets it on the ground, and rolls the Bullet back a few feet.

The fountain bursts into a shower of light.

MARTY (delighted)
All *right*!

276 EXT.   THE SLOPE OF THE CUT, MEDIUM LONG   276

The waterfall is in the b.g.

The WEREWOLF is climbing the rocky slope.

277 EXT.   THE FOUNTAIN, CU   277

It goes out.

278 EXT.   MARTY   278

He rolls over to the picnic table and gets a Roman candle. He plants the stick in the ground and lights the fuse. The Roman candle shoots into the sky.

279 EXT.   THE ROMAN CANDLE   279

Bursts into colored light.

280 EXT.   THE WEREWOLF, NEAR THE TOP OF THE CUT, MEDIUM   280
LONG
It GROWLS...and shakes its fists at the fading light in the sky.

281 EXT.   MARTY   281

He's holding another fountain in one hand and his matches in the other. He's looking toward the cut and the waterfall.

MARTY
Is someone there?

282 EXT.   THE WEREWOLF, NEAR THE TOP OF THE CUT   282

It freezes, GROWLING FAINTLY.

283 EXT.   MARTY   283

With a little shrug, he lights the fuse on the fountain and sets it on the ground, as before.

284 EXT.   THE BACK OF THE GROVE, AT THE TOP OF THE CUT   284

Claw-hands settle over the top.

214

285 EXT.   THE FOUNTAIN, CU   285

It throws off fiery swirls of sparks, then begins to die down.

286 EXT.   MARTY   286

He's checking out the stuff on the table for his next choice when he
hears a clear SOUND: A SNAPPING, SPLINTERING BRANCH.

287 EXT.   THE GROVE, WITH THE WEREWOLF   287

It's run into a low-hanging branch. Instead of pushing it aside or
ducking under it, it simply rips it off the tree. Although the branch is
pretty big, the WEREWOLF does this as easily as a hungry man
might rip a drumstick off a Thanksgiving turkey. It throws the
branch aside and advances, hunched over on two legs.

288 EXT.   MARTY   288

                         MARTY (terrified)
            Who's there?

289 EXT.   THE GROVE AT THE BACK OF THE REST AREA, MARTY'S   289
    POV
The grove is a darkened shadowland.

290 EXT.   MARTY   290

He punches the Bullet's starter. The motor cranks and cranks. No go,
though. MARTY pulls out the choke wire, alternating terrified stares
at the grove of trees with terrified stares at his rudimentary
dashboard.

291 EXT.   THE GROVE, MARTY'S POV   291

Here *it* comes, out of the shadows, closing in.

292 EXT.   MARTY   292

Working that starter for all it's worth . . . but the motor only cranks.
Still no start.

293 EXT.   CLAWED, FURRY FEET   293

294 EXT.   MARTY   294

He gives up on the motor. He looks toward the picnic table where
his fireworks are. He grabs up the tracer. He gets the matches out of
the breast pocket of his p.j.'s and promptly drops them in his lap.
He scrabbles for them.

295 EXT.   THE WEREWOLF, MARTY'S POV   295

We can't see its face in the dark, but it's closer . . . much closer.

296 EXT. MARTY   296

He tries to hold the tracer and strike a match at the same time. He
can't; to do that he'd need at least one more hand. He puts the tube
of the tracer between his teeth and tries again.

297 EXT. THE MATCHBOOK AND MARTY'S HANDS   297

He strikes the match . . . too hard! It bends, its neck broken.

MARTY (voice; moaning)
Oh, please . . .

298 EXT. WEREWOLF CLAWS, OPENING AND CLOSING   298

299 EXT. MARTY   299

He is in an extremity of terror.

300 EXT. THE MATCHBOOK AND MARTY'S HANDS, CU   300

He pulls a fresh match from the book and strikes it. It lights.

301 EXT. THE WEREWOLF   301

It recoils—we still can't see its face except for a vague shape.

[NOTE: I keep emphasizing the shadowed face, because this is *not* a
full-moon period. I've been going on the assumption that the guy
kind of works his way up to full wolfiness, toothiness, hairiness,
etc., starting with a partial change at about the second quarter. It's a
process like the tide coming in. Thus, if we saw MARTY'S attacker
clearly at this point, I think we would recognize him.]

302 EXT. MARTY, IN THE SILVER BULLET   302

He takes the tracer from his mouth and applies the match to the
fuse. It splutters alight.

303 EXT. MARTY AND THE WEREWOLF, A WIDER SHOT   303

The WEREWOLF is less than twenty feet away. The tracer flares
alight and shoots out of MARTY'S hand, leaving a pink-orange trail
of smoke behind it. The missile flies at the WEREWOLF'S head.

304 EXT. THE WEREWOLF   304

The tracer strikes it in the face, and we see a flash of fire. The
WEREWOLF screams and blunders away.

305 EXT. MARTY, IN THE SILVER BULLET   305

He punches the starter again. The motor cranks.

306 EXT.   THE MOTOR OF THE SILVER BULLET   306

The motor coughs and fires; a big blue flame jumps from the fancy carb . . . and the engine starts to run.

307 EXT.   THE WEREWOLF   307

It's staggering away, ROARING and HOWLING. The tube of the tracer is sticking out of its face—from its left eye, in fact—like an Indian's arrow. The WEREWOLF smashes branches out of its way.

308 EXT.   MARTY IN THE SILVER BULLET   308

He wheels the Bullet around and heads for the road, gasping and weeping with fear.

309 EXT.   THE WEREWOLF, IN THE GROVE   309

It's blundering through the trees. It pulls the tube from its face with an ANIMAL SCREAM and drops it.

310 EXT.   THE TRACER, CU   310

It lies smoldering on the ground. The end is slick with blood.

311 EXT.   THE ROAD, WITH MARTY   311

The Bullet is really wheeling. MARTY is panting, out of breath, still deeply frightened.

312 EXT.   THE WOODS, WITH THE WEREWOLF   312

We see it blundering along, holding its face; blood bubbles through its fingers.

                    WEREWOLF (snarling voice)
         Bastard Marty! Bastard Marty! Kill you! Reeeal slow!

313 EXT.   COSLAW DRIVEWAY, WITH MARTY   313

He powers up it, and along the path to the back. Perhaps he has enough speed to cut the engine and coast.

314 INT.   MARTY'S BEDROOM   314

His bed is by the window. His hands appear on the windowsill, and Marty pulls himself in. He falls over onto his bed and lies there, spent and exhausted and trembling.

315 EXT.   THE COSLAW HOUSE, VERY EARLY MORNING   315
SOUND: RINGING TELEPHONE (FILTER)

316   INT.   THE COSLAW LIVING ROOM, WITH MARTY   316

He's sitting in the "house" wheelchair in the living room, holding
the phone tensely to his ear as the RINGING SOUND goes on.

A CLICK as the phone is picked up.

                    UNCLE AL (muzzy voice)
            'Lo? Go away.

                    MARTY
            It *is* a werewolf! I *saw* it! Last night—

317   INT.   UNCLE AL'S BEDROOM   317

Not a really spiffy place—the decor is Early American Alcoholic.
There's a mostly unclad lady asleep on one side of the bed. UNCLE
AL is sitting on the other in his skivvies, phone to his ear. There are
a lot of bottles and heaped ashtrays around, and UNCLE AL has a
big old hangover.

                    UNCLE AL
            You dreamed it, Marty.

                    MARTY (voice)
            No! I went out late last night—and—

                    UNCLE AL
            There are no such things as werewolves. Please,
            dear boy, have some pity.

He hangs up and falls back into bed.

                    GIRL (muzzy voice)
            Whowuzzit?

                    UNCLE AL
            Obscene phone caller. Go back to sleep.

318   EXT.   THE BACK PORCH, WITH MARTY   318

He's sitting on the Silver Bullet, just looking at the yard. JANE
comes out.

                    JANE
            Marty? You okay? You've just been sitting here all
            morning.

                    MARTY
            Where's Mom?

                    JANE
            Went shopping. Why?

                    MARTY
            Janey, I have to talk to you.

                   JANE (mistrustfully)
About what?

MARTY looks at her earnestly.

                   MARTY
I need you to help me. Uncle Al won't believe me,
and if you won't help me, I...I...

MARTY has to stop. He's almost crying.

                   JANE (concerned)
Marty, what *is* it?

319 EXT.   MAIN STREET, MEDIUM LONG, WITH JANE   319

JANE is pushing a supermarket shopping cart with a lot of beer and
soda bottles in it. On the side is a sign reading MEDCU BOTTLE AND
CAN DRIVE—plus an outline drawing of the Medcu unit.

                   JANE (voice-over)
He told me something that was clearly unbelievable
...and yet, somehow I believed most of it. And I
understood one thing with total clarity: Marty
himself believed it *all*.

She turns into a yard and pulls her cart up the walk to the door. She
mounts the steps and rings the bell.

320 EXT.   THE PORCH, WITH JANE, A CLOSER SHOT.   320

A sheer curtain at one side of the door is pulled aside and a fearful
face—that of MRS. THAYER—looks out. Then we hear bolts being
pulled and locks—at least three of them—being unlocked. The lady
is taking no chances.

                   MRS. THAYER
      Jane?

                   JANE (politely)
I'm collecting returnable bottles and cans for the
Medcu Drive, Missus Thayer—I just wondered if
you had any.

Her husband comes up the hall.

                   MR. THAYER
      Who is it?

                   MRS. THAYER
      Jane Coslaw.

321 EXT.   JANE, CU   321

What we see mostly are her eyes—bright, inquiring.

JANE
Hi, Mr. Thayer.

322 INT.   LON THAYER, ECU   322

What we see mostly are his brown eyes.

THAYER
Hello, Jane.

323 EXT.   THE PORCH, WITH JANE AND MRS. THAYER   323

MRS. THAYER
Bring your cart around to the back, Jane—we'll
look in the garage.

JANE
Thank you.

She starts down the steps and we

DISSOLVE TO:

324 EXT.   JANE, ON MAIN STREET   DAY   324

Amazing how deserted Tarker's Mills looks. JANE is pushing her
cart. Even more bottles in it now.

JANE (voice-over)
Uncle Al hadn't believed him, but Uncle Al was
thirty-five that summer and I was fourteen . . . at
fourteen you can still believe the unbelievable,
although even then that ability is growing rusty, is
preparing to squeal to a stop.

She is passing the Holy Family rectory. LESTER LOWE is out front,
digging in his flower garden. He is shirtless, back to JANE and to us;
his black shirt with the turned-around collar hangs informally on a
bush.

JANE (calls)
Hi, Father Lowe!

LOWE (without turning)
Top of the morning to you, Jane Coslaw!

JANE
I'm going to bring in a *monster* load of bottles in an
hour or so!

LOWE (still digging)
That's great, Jane . . . I'll be waiting.

325 EXT.   JANE, FARTHER DOWN MAIN STREET   325

She stops at Robertson's Luncheonette, leaves her cart outside, and
goes in. THE CAMERA FLOATS TO THE WINDOW; we see JANE

explaining about the bottle campaign to BOBBY while a few men
seated at the counter listen.

326 INT.   JANE, ECU   326

Wide eyes, mostly.

327 INT.   BOBBY ROBERTSON, ECU   327

Mostly eyes.

328 INT.   ROBERTSON'S, FEATURING JANE   328

As she turns away, her eyes sweep the men at the counter.

329 INT.   THE MEN, JANE'S POV   329

Some of them—PELTZER, VIRGIL, CUTTS—are familiar. Others are
not. THE CAMERA PANS THEIR FACES CLOSELY, FEATURING
THEIR EYES.

330 EXT.   OUTSIDE ROBERTSON'S, WITH JANE   330

She grabs the handle of the cart again and proceeds down Main
Street. She goes into the barber shop.

> JANE (v-o)
> Marty had seen where the tracer had struck home,
> he said, and I went out that day doing more than
> just looking for returnable cans and bottles—I was
> looking for a man—or woman—with only one eye.

331 INT.   THE BARBER SHOP   DAY   331

As JANE enters, BILLY McCLAREN is giving one man a trim.
Another man is tipped back with his face wrapped in a towel. Two
or three other townies are waiting on tonsorial beautification, reading
magazines. None, of course, has only one eye. JANE checks them all
out carefully.

> BILLY
> I know what you're after, Jane, and you're out of
> luck. Little Toby Whittislaw was in yesterday, and I
> gave 'em all to him.
> JANE
> Oh . . . okay.

But her eyes have fixed on the towel over the face of the man in the
other barber chair. She walks over to him.

332 INT.   JANE AND THE TOWELED MAN, CLOSER ON   332

> JANE
> That you, Mr. Fairton?

> ANDY FAIRTON (muffled)
> No—it's Ronald McDonald. I came in for a shave
> and a burger.

The men laugh. JANE smiles politely. And pulls the hot towel away
from his eyes. His *two* eyes.

> JANE (sweetly)
> Got any bottles, Mr. Fairton?

> ANDY
> *No!*

> JANE (just as sweet)
> Oh . . . okay.

She puts the towel back and THE CAMERA FOLLOWS as she
returns to the door.

> JANE
> 'Bye, Mr. McClaren.

> BILLY (amused)
> 'Bye, Jane.

> ANDY (muffled)
> Jesus!

JANE goes out.

333   EXT.   JANE, AT THE RECTORY   333

She pushes the shopping cart up to the gate, opens it, and goes up
the walk to the foot of LOWE'S porch steps. She leaves it there and
climbs to the porch.

334   EXT.   JANE, ON THE PORCH   334

The screen door is shut, the inner wooden door open.

335   INT.   THE RECTORY HALLWAY, JANE'S POV   335

Dark and empty. SOUNDS in the kitchen. EATING SOUNDS,
maybe—or maybe we can't tell.

336   EXT.   JANE, ON THE PORCH   336

She knocks on the screen door.

> JANE
> Father Lowe? I'm ready to turn in my bottles and
> cans!

337   INT.   THE KITCHEN   337

LOWE is standing by the refrigerator door. He's holding a raw leg of
lamb and tearing at it with his teeth. Lamb blood smears his face and

runs down his arms. He is as human as you or me (in a manner of speaking, as UNCLE AL would say), but when JANE speaks, his head snaps up and his eye flares—his one eye. The other is covered by a patch.

> JANE (voice)
> Father?

> LOWE
> Take your cart around to the garage and unload, Jane! Then bring me your tally sheet!

338 EXT.   JANE, ON THE PORCH   338

> JANE
> Okay!

She goes down the steps and begins to push the cart around the house.

339 EXT.   JANE, A WIDER SHOT   339

She goes down the steps and starts to push the cart around the house.

340 INT.   THE KITCHEN, WITH LOWE   340

He crosses to the window over the kitchen sink, the bloody chunk of meat still in his hands, and looks out.

341 EXT.   JANE, LOWE'S POV   341

She pushes the cart along a path toward a combination garage and utility shed at the back.

342 INT.   THE KITCHEN, WITH LOWE   342

Still watching JANE, he begins to gnaw ravenously at the meat again.

343 EXT.   JANE, AT THE SHED-GARAGE   343

She opens the door and slowly pushes her cart inside.

344 INT.   THE UTILITY SHED-GARAGE, WITH JANE   344

This is a creepy little place, now filled with bottles and cans that have been crammed in helter-skelter, every which way. JANE obviously doesn't like it. She begins to unload her cart rapidly, mumbling numbers to herself.

SOUND: SQUEAKING.

JANE looks down.

345 INT.   THE UTILITY SHED-GARAGE FLOOR, JANE'S POV   345

A good-sized mouse comes out from between a pile of stacked
bottles and runs across JANE'S shoe.

346 INT.   JANE   346

She utters a little scream and shrinks back against the wall, bumping
it quite hard. Hard enough to knock something off an overhead
shelf. It falls into the bottles, SHATTERING several. JANE screams
again—not terribly loud—and then slowly bends toward the object
and picks it up.

JANE holds it, both puzzled and scared.

347 EXT.   THE BACK DOOR OF THE RECTORY   347

JANE approaches it, holding a piece of paper in one hand—her tally
sheet. She knocks. Waits. There is no answer. She knocks again.
Waits. No answer. She tries the door. It opens.

                              JANE
                    Father Lowe?

No answer. After a moment of interior debate, JANE enters the
kitchen.

348 INT.   JANE, IN THE RECTORY KITCHEN   348

She looks around. No one here. But there is a bloody spot on the
counter—LOWE must have set his grisly luncheon down here for a
moment. She walks slowly across the kitchen and into the dark hall.

                              JANE
                    Father Lowe?... I've got my tally sheet...

Farther into the hall. A hand drops onto her shoulder.

                         LOWE (voice)
                    Very good, Jane!

She jumps, and so do we. She turns around and looks up at:

349 INT.   FATHER LOWE, ECU   349

Featuring his eyes—his *eye*, rather. The left is covered with a black
eye-patch.

                         LOWE (grins)
                    Good, Jane. Very... very good.

He holds his hand out, and JANE puts the tally sheet in it like one
in a dream. She can't take her eyes off that black patch, which tells
her everything.

224

350 INT.   THE HALLWAY, WITH JANE AND LOWE   350

>   LOWE (concerned)
> Jane! You're trembling!
>
>   JANE
> I . . . I don't feel so well, I guess maybe I got too
> much sun.
>
>   LOWE
> Would you like to come in the parlor and lie down
> for a bit? Or have a cold drink? I have some soda—
>
>   JANE
> *No!* (softer) That is, I have to get home and help
> my mom with lunch.
>
>   LOWE
> I'll give you a ride!

JANE is retreating down the hall toward the front door.

>   JANE
> No—she . . . she was going to meet me at the
> market. I'll be fine.

351 INT.   LOWE, CU   351

How much does he know? How much has he guessed? Hard to tell
from his face, which now seems sinister, with its eye-patch.

>   LOWE
> Give my best to your brother, Jane.

352 INT.   JANE, AT THE PORCH END OF THE HALLWAY   352

>   JANE
> I will!

She bolts.

353 INT.   LOWE, IN THE HALLWAY   353

CAMERA HOLDS ON HIM, standing silent and enigmatic.

>   LOWE (soft)
> Real slow.

354 EXT.   THE COSLAW BACKYARD, WITH MARTY   354

His eyes are wide. He's leaning forward in his wheelchair.

>   MARTY (almost moaning)
> Oh, *Jeez!* What did you do then?

355 EXT.   JANE AND MARTY   355

She's changed into shorts and a blouse.

> JANE
> I ran faster than I ever ran in my life—what do you
> think, dummox? By the time I got back here, I
> really thought I *was* going to faint. (Pause) What are
> we going to do, Marty? If we tried to tell
> anybody—grown-ups, I mean—they'd laugh.
> What are we going to do?

> MARTY (thoughtfully)
> I think I know.

356 INT.   A SHEET OF RULED SCHOOL NOTEBOOK PAPER, CU   356

A hand—MARTY'S—comes into the frame and prints: I KNOW WHO
YOU ARE, AND I KNOW *WHAT* YOU ARE.

357 INT.   MARTY'S ROOM, WITH MARTY   357

He's sitting at his desk, a pool of light from the lamp focused on the
sheet of paper before him. He thinks a moment, then begins to write
again.

358 INT.   THE NOTEBOOK PAD, CU   358

He is adding: WHY DON'T YOU KILL YOURSELF?

359 INT.   MARTY, AT HIS DESK   359

He studies this for a second, and seems satisfied. He opens a
drawer, brings out an envelope, and folds his letter into it.

360 EXT.   JANE, ON MAIN STREET   360

She has the letter in her hand. She approaches the mailbox, opens
the mailbox door, and then glances at the envelope again.

361 EXT.   THE ENVELOPE, JANE'S POV   361

Addressed in pencil, it says: FATHER LESTER LOWE/HOLY FAMILY RECTORY/
149 MAIN STREET/TARKER'S MILLS, MAINE.

362 EXT.   JANE, AT THE MAILBOX   362

She drops the letter in with the air of a girl lighting the fuse on a
packet of high explosive. She turns away toward home.

363 INT.   THE RECTORY LIVING ROOM, WITH LESTER LOWE   363

He's standing at the window and looking out. The torn-open
envelope is on an end table beside him. He's holding the lined sheet

of paper in his hand. An expression of bitter hate twists his features, and he slowly crumples the paper in his fist.

364   EXT.   JANE, AT THE MAIN STREET MAILBOX   364

She drops in another letter and walks away.

                          JANE (v-o)
          I mailed another letter for Marty the next day...a
          third the day after that. Then, on Saturday...

365   EXT.   THE TARKER'S MILLS TOWN COMMON, LONG   365

Parked at the curb is UNCLE AL'S sports car.

                          JANE (v-o)
          ...we told Uncle Al what we'd been up to. (Pause)
          His reaction was less than serene.

366   EXT.   UNCLE AL, JANE, AND MARTY, ON THE COMMON 366
                          UNCLE AL
          Holy-jumped-up-baldheaded-Jesus-CHRIST!
                          JANE
          Uncle Al—

                          UNCLE AL (to JANE)
          From *him* I'd expect it. I sometimes think his
          common sense got paralyzed along with his legs.
          But *you,* Jane! *You!* Little Polly Practical!

                          JANE (quiet)
          You don't understand.

                          UNCLE AL (wildly)
          Oh, I understand *plenty*! I understand that my niece
          and nephew are sending the local Catholic priest
          little love notes suggesting that he gargle with a
          broken light bulb or eat a rat-poison omelet!

                          MARTY
          It *came* for me! I shot it in the eye! Now *he's*
          wearing an eye-patch!

                          UNCLE AL
          I called Peltzer on my way over here, Marty. Father
          Lowe came into the drugstore two days ago for a
          bottle of otic solution. That's a fancy way of saying
          eyewash. He's got a corneal inflammation.

                          MARTY
          Was it a prescription?

227

UNCLE AL
What the hell does *that* matter?

MARTY
It wasn't—I'll bet you it wasn't. Because to get a
prescription he'd have to see a doctor.

UNCLE AL
Marty, Marty, you should hear yourself!

MARTY
Well . . . *was* it a prescription?

UNCLE AL
I don't know. But I know you didn't see any
werewolf the other night, Marty. You had a dream,
that's all. An extremely realistic nightmare brought
on by what's been happening in this town.

MARTY
What about the baseball bat Jane saw in his shed?
You know who used to have a baseball bat like
that? Mr. Knopfler! He was so proud of it he used
to carry it in the Fourth of July parade! Jane said it
looked like the Green Giant used it for a toothpick!

UNCLE AL
You want to know what I think?

MARTY
No—we just got you out here so we could admire
your pretty face.

UNCLE AL
Watch it, dear boy. I think it was a hallucination.
Probably a broomstick, or something.

JANE (indignant)
It was *not*! You want me to show you? Come on!
I'm not afraid! I'll show you right now!

UNCLE AL
No thank you, Jane. I'm a little too old for playing
the Hardy Boys Meet the Catholic Werewolf.

JANE stamps her foot, furious with UNCLE AL.

MARTY
Never mind, Jane. He'll have gotten rid of it by
now anyway.

367 EXT.   OUTSIDE OF ROBERTSON'S LUNCHEONETTE   367

The Silver Bullet stands outside. The door opens and UNCLE AL,
JANE, and MARTY come out. UNCLE AL is carrying MARTY
piggyback. MARTY has an ice cream cone. JANE is holding two.

228

UNCLE AL squats, depositing MARTY in the Bullet. MARTY starts the engine as JANE hands UNCLE AL his ice cream cone. The three of them start up the street and THE CAMERA TRACKS THEM.

> JANE
> If Father Lowe is just an innocent little lamb, why hasn't he picked up the telephone and called Constable Haller to tell him Marty's sending poison-pen letters?

> UNCLE AL
> I don't accept the idea that he knows who his letter writer is, Jane. Because I don't accept the idea that there was a big bad wolf who saw Marty in his wheelchair.

> JANE
> Why hasn't he picked up the telephone and told Constable Haller that *someone* is sending him poison-pen letters?

UNCLE AL stops. He hasn't thought of this. He looks toward:

368   EXT.   THE CATHOLIC RECTORY, LONG—UNCLE AL'S POV   368

LESTER LOWE is mowing the lawn, eye-patch and all.

369   EXT.   MAIN STREET, WITH UNCLE AL, MARTY, AND JANE   369

> UNCLE AL (a bit perplexed)
> Well . . . he probably did. I mean, he could make a complaint without taking an ad out in the paper, couldn't he?

> MARTY
> I'll bet you a quarter that eyewash stuff was nonprescription. And I'll bet you another quarter he hasn't said anything to Mr. Haller.

> UNCLE AL
> Marty, do you see your suspect?

370   EXT.   THE RECTORY LAWN, WITH LESTER LOWE   370

Keeps on mowing. MR. ASPINALL drives by and waves. LOWE waves back.

371   EXT.   MAIN STREET, WITH UNCLE AL, MARTY, AND JANE   371

> MARTY (grim) Yes, I see him.

> UNCLE AL
> Do you really think that a man who took a rocket in the eye three nights ago could be out mowing his lawn? He'd either be in the hospital . . . or dead.

MARTY

I didn't shoot him when he was a *man*. I shot him
when he was—

UNCLE AL

When he was a werewolf. Yes. Right. Jesus. Jane,
you don't really believe this madness, do you?

JANE

I don't know exactly *what* I believe. But I *know* that
what I saw was a baseball bat and not a
broomstick. I *know* there was something strange
about the way the house smelled that day. It
smelled like an animal's den. And I believe in
Marty. I mean—there are times when he makes me
so mad I could kill him, but I still believe in him.
(Pause) You used to believe in him, too, Uncle Al.

UNCLE AL looks momentarily ashamed of himself. Then he throws
his hands up in disgust.

UNCLE AL

Kids!

He walks ahead of them, MARTY bats his eyes sweetly at JANE.

She walks on, miffed. MARTY gooses the Silver Bullet to catch up.

372   EXT.   A FIELD ON THE OUTSKIRTS OF TOWN   DAY   372

It's midafternoon. A bunch of kids are playing baseball. In the
extreme f.g. we see one small boy—MARTY—sitting back to us in
his wheelchair, watching.

373   EXT.   AN OLD COUPE   373

It draws slowly along a tree-lined lane and stops. LESTER LOWE is
behind the wheel.

SOUNDS OF THE BASEBALL GAME CONTINUE.

374   EXT.   THE BASEBALL FIELD, AND MARTY, LOWE'S POV   374

THE CAMERA MOVES SLOWLY IN ON MARTY'S BACK.

375   EXT.   LESTER LOWE   375

LOWE (quietly)

Little bastard.

376   EXT.   A FLY BALL   376

377   EXT.   THE FIELD, A WIDER SHOT   377

The field team heads in. Kids start streaming back toward town.

378 EXT.   MARTY   378

The OUTFIELDER who caught the fly trots past, and glances his
way.

                          OUTFIELDER
           You comin' down to Robertson's for a soda, Marty?
                          MARTY
           No—I guess I'll go home.

I think that here we are seeing a rare moment of depression in
MARTY—they can run and play ball. He can't.
                          OUTFIELDER
           Okay—seeya!
                          MARTY
           Yeah . . . seeya.

He fires up the Bullet and starts away alone.

379 EXT.   LOWE'S COUPE   379

He starts it up.

380 EXT.   MARTY, LOWE'S POV   380

He bumps up a grassy slope to a tarred road. The last of the other
kids are headed back the other way. MARTY is alone.

381 EXT.   LOWE'S COUPE   381

It turns out of the lane where it was parked and onto the road.

382 EXT.   MARTY'S WHEELCHAIR, LOWE'S POV   382

MARTY'S back is to us. The wheelchair draws rapidly closer to THE
CAMERA as LOWE bears down on it.

383 INT.   LOWE, BEHIND THE COUPE'S WHEEL   383

He leans over the wheel, grinning sadistically.
                          LOWE (whispers)
           Bastard.

384 EXT.   MARTY, IN THE SILVER BULLET   384

He's daydreaming his way along—maybe, inside his head, he's
playing center field for the Dodgers.

SOUND: Winding roar of a car engine. MARTY turns around.

385 EXT.   LOWE'S COUPE, MARTY'S POV, ROARING AT THE   385
CAMERA.

386 EXT.   MARTY AND LOWE'S COUPE   386

MARTY opens the throttle wide and the Bullet swerves across the
road. The coupe's bumper actually clips it on the way by, jolting
MARTY and almost overturning the Bullet.

LOWE'S coupe veers over the embankment and partway down into
the ditch.

387 INT.   LOWE, BEHIND THE WHEEL OF THE COUPE   387
                         LOWE
               Oh, you bastard!

He floors the engine.

388 EXT.   THE COUPE'S REAR WHEELS   388

Spinning helplessly in the dirt.

389 EXT.   MARTY, IN THE SILVER BULLET   389

He speeds past the coupe, and thumbs his nose.

390 INT.   LOWE, IN THE COUPE   390

He's in a teeth-grinding fury. He jams the gear shift lever into
reverse and floors the gas pedal again.

391 EXT.   THE COUPE   391

It roars backward in a cloud of ditch dust and bounces onto the
road. Then it screams out after the rapidly disappearing Silver Bullet.

392 EXT.   THE SILVER BULLET, WITH MARTY   392

He hears the GROWING SOUND of LESTER LOWE'S coupe. He
looks behind.

393 EXT.   THE COUPE   393

Roars toward THE CAMERA

394 EXT.   MARTY, IN THE SILVER BULLET   394

He twists the throttle and the Silver Bullet responds.

395 EXT.   CHASE MONTAGE   395

The director will shoot it as he likes—the basis is simple: LOWE is
chasing MARTY'S hopped-up wheelchair along a country road at
speeds approaching fifty MPH. MARTY should have a couple of near
misses, and perhaps we could actually have him *pass* one car. At one
point we should have a REVERSE ANGLE on LESTER LOWE'S

coupe, featuring two bumper stickers: ATTEND AND SUPPORT YOUR LOCAL CHURCH and HONK IF YOU LOVE JESUS!

As the chase goes on it becomes apparent that LOWE is gaining. MARTY looks increasingly desperate. And now he looks down at:

396   EXT.   THE SILVER BULLET'S GAS GAUGE, MARTY'S POV   396

The needle is all the way over on E.

397   EXT.   MARTY   397

He groans. SOUND of the coupe's engine GROWS LOUDER.

398   EXT.   THE COUPE AND THE SILVER BULLET   398

LOWE charges, rapidly closing the distance. MARTY swerves from one side of the road to the other, escaping LOWE for the moment but almost overturning in the process.

They are now running beside a river—the Auger River, in fact.

399   EXT.   THE BULLET'S GAS GAUGE   399

Now the needle is actually *past E.*

400   EXT.   MARTY   400

MARTY
Come on, baby . . . come on . . .

His face registers hope as he sees:

401   EXT.   ROADSIDE SIGN, MARTY'S POV   401

AUGER RIVER COVERED BRIDGE 2000 FEET AHEAD *AUTOMOBILES PROHIBITED!*

402   EXT.   MARTY, IN THE BULLET   402

He twists the throttle as far as it will turn—he's going for broke. The coupe chases him—and now the Silver Bullet's motor COUGHS.

403   EXT.   THE BRIDGE, MARTY'S POV   403

It's pretty ramshackle. A big orange sign beside it reads: BRIDGE UNSAFE! TRUCKS AND AUTOS ABSOLUTELY PROHIBITED!

404   EXT.   THE SILVER BULLET   404

MARTY brakes, hits the shoulder of the road, and somehow makes the turn. We see him holding on for dear life as the Silver Bullet bounces and jounces down the dirt road to the mouth of the covered bridge.

405 EXT.   LOWE'S COUPE   405

It overshoots the right turn MARTY just took, screeches to a halt, backs up, and turns onto the lane.

406 EXT.   THE SILVER BULLET   406

It bounces up the incline to the bridge, MOTOR COUGHING AND SPLUTTERING.

407 EXT.   THE COUPE   407

It comes to a sliding, dirt-digging stop.

408 INT.   LOWE, BEHIND THE WHEEL.   408

His face is so full of frustrated hate that it has become the face of a gargoyle.

409 EXT.   THE SIGN PROHIBITING MOTOR TRAFFIC, LOWE'S POV   409

410 EXT./INT.   THE COVERED BRIDGE, WITH THE BULLET   410

It's dim and spooky in here. Cracks between the boards of the side walls allow dusty fingers of daylight to shine through. More light rays up from the cracks in the floor. The floorboards are warped and uneven; MARTY'S wheelchair sways drunkenly from side to side. The total inside passage is about seventy feet.

About halfway across, the Silver Bullet coughs its last cough and splutters its last splutter. It rolls along silently, going on its dying momentum.

411 EXT.   THE FAR END OF THE BRIDGE, MARTY'S POV   411

Drawing closer. We hear the SOUNDS of boards rumbling under the Silver Bullet's tires and the Auger River beneath.

412 EXT.   MARTY, REVERSE   412

Rolling ever more slowly, the Silver Bullet approaches THE CAMERA ...and stops. MARTY is covered with sweat. His hair is in a wild tangle. He's panting. He looks at:

413 EXT.   THE LANE LEADING AWAY FROM THE BRIDGE, MARTY'S   413
POV

This is an extremely rustic lane. Pretty, but hardly the sort of place in which one would want to find oneself when one has a part-time werewolf and a full-time homicidal maniac close behind.

414 EXT.   MARTY, AT THE MOUTH OF THE BRIDGE   414
                          LOWE (soft voice)
              Marty...

MARTY's head whips around.

415 EXT.   THE FAR END OF THE BRIDGE, MARTY'S POV   415

We see a brilliant square of light. In it stands LOWE'S silhouette. The
silouette begins to move. SOUND of footfalls on the loose
floorboards of the covered bridge.

416 INT.   LOWE'S SHOES   416

Sensible black Oxfords.

                          LOWE
              I'm very sorry about this. I don't know if you
              believe that or not, but it's true. I would never
              willingly hurt a child. You should have left me
              alone, Marty.

SOUND of footfalls resumes.

417 EXT.   MARTY   417

He's nearly paralyzed with terror—even if he wasn't, he wouldn't
get far in a powerless Silver Bullet.

418 INT.   LOWE, IN THE SHADOWS   418
                          LOWE (soft; soothing)
              I *can't* kill myself, Marty. You see, our religion
              teaches that suicide is the greatest sin a man or a
              woman can commit. Stella Randolph was going to
              commit suicide; if she had done so, she would be
              burning in hell right now. By killing her I took her
              physical life but saved her life eternal. You see,
              Marty? You see how all things serve the will and
              the mind of God? You see, you meddling little *shit*!

He begins to walk forward again.

419 EXT.   LOWE, MARTY'S POV   419

He's halfway across the bridge now, walking slowly, not hurrying.
                          LOWE
              You're going to have a terrible accident, Marty.
              You're going to fall into the river.
SOUND: TRACTOR ENGINE, LOWE stops, alert to possible danger.

420 EXT.   MARTY   420

TRACTOR SOUND IS LOUDER.

MARTY'S face fills with hope. He looks from LOWE toward:

421 EXT.   THE LANE, MARTY'S POV   421

THE TRACTOR SOUND gets louder still, and here comes ELMER
ZINNEMAN on a John Deere. The tractor is hauling a manure
spreader which is mostly empty.

422 EXT.   MARTY   422

MARTY (waving madly)
Mr. Zinneman! Mr. Zinneman!

423 INT.   THE COVERED BRIDGE, WITH LOWE   423

He draws back a little, and his face is sharp with animal cunning—
inside his head he's running a four-minute mile. Stay and try to bluff
it out, or beat it?

424 EXT.   ELMER AND MARTY   424

ELMER draws the tractor up close to MARTY and swings it around.
MARTY looks back at:

425 INT.   THE COVERED BRIDGE, MARTY'S POV   425

Empty.

SOUND OF A CAR STARTING, FAINT.

426 EXT.   MARTY AND ELMER   426

MARTY looks back at ELMER

MARTY
I ran out of gas.

ELMER
Spooky in there, ennit?

MARTY (with feeling)
It sure is!

He looks back once more toward:

427 EXT./INT.   THE COVERED BRIDGE, MARTY'S POV   427

Brooding, shadowy. CAMERA HOLDS AND WE

DISSOLVE TO:

MARTY is talking to UNCLE AL. JANE is behind them, knocking croquet balls through the wickets on the back lawn.

MARTY is looking at his Uncle anxiously as JANE strolls over.

                    UNCLE AL
Well . . . it's a lot easier to swallow without the hair
and the foaming jaws. Also, I checked on the otic
solution. It was counter brand. No prescription
needed.

                    MARTY
I *told* you!

                    UNCLE AL
Shut up, dear boy—no gloating allowed.

                    JANE (sits down)
Did you talk to the constable?

                    UNCLE AL
After Marty called me with this latest Thrilling Tale
of Wonder, I did. (Pause) He's had no poison-pen
complaints lodged at all.

                    MARTY
I told you!

                    JANE
Shut up, Marty.

                    UNCLE AL (reluctantly)
There's something else.

MARTY   JANE
What is it?   What other thing?

                    UNCLE AL
I probably shouldn't tell you—you're both hysterical
on the subject. I'm starting to feel like a guy handing
out free Arthur Murray coupons to victims of the
dancing sickness.

                    MARTY
Uncle Al, if you don't tell me—

He makes strangling gestures.

                    UNCLE AL (reluctant)
I went out to that rest area.

                    MARTY (triumph)
You found the tracer!

UNCLE AL
No . . . but I found some blood, smeared on a tree
trunk in that grove.

MARTY
There! You see!

UNCLE AL
It could have been anything, Marty.

MARTY
What about Father Lowe chasing me in his car and
trying to run me down? You don't think *that* was a
dream, do you?

UNCLE AL
No.

UNCLE AL comes over to JANE's side of the Silver Bullet. He looks
down at:

429 EXT.   THE FRAME OF THE BULLET   429

There's a scrape and a dent where LOWE'S coupe dented it. There is
also a fleck of paint.

430 EXT.   UNCLE AL AND JANE, CUT   430

UNCLE AL
Lowe's car—?

JANE
Blue. *This* blue.

UNCLE AL
Jesus.

431 EXT.   THE NIGHT SKY, WITH THE MOON   431

Three-quarters full.

THE CAMERA PANS DOWN to the Tarker's Mills town hall. UNCLE
AL'S sportster is parked out front.

432 EXT.   THE CONSTABLE'S OFFICE, WITH HALLER AND UNCLE   432
AL

HALLER is behind his desk, rocked back in his chair, hands laced
together behind his head. He's looking at UNCLE AL. There's a
silence that draws out for quite some time. In it, UNCLE AL
becomes steadily more uncomfortable.

HALLER
That's just about the craziest damn story I've ever
heard, Al.

238

UNCLE AL
I know. I could have edited out all of the *completely*
crazy stuff, but I thought you deserved to hear it
with the bark on.

HALLER
I appreciate that. Now, the next question: Do you
believe any of this? You do, don't you?

UNCLE AL
Let's just say I believe Lester Lowe should be
checked out.

HALLER rises.

HALLER
That can be arranged.

They shake hands.

433   EXT.   THE RECTORY   NIGHT   433

A Chevrolet with TARKER'S MILLS CONSTABLE painted on the side in
gold leaf pulls up. JOE HALLER gets out, and as he does there's a
business of pulling his pants legs down over his boots — nice stitched
cowboy boots, not black cop's shoes. We want the audience to notice
these boots, remember them — probably HALLER should wear them
all through the picture. He goes up the walk.

HALLER rings the doorbell.

No one comes. HALLER rings the bell again. Waits. No one comes.
He leans down and looks through a side window.

434   INT.   THE RECTORY HALL AND SITTING ROOM, HALLER'S   434
       POV

No one there.

435   EXT.   HALLER   435

He goes down the steps, stands on the path for a moment, and then
goes over to the shed-garage. He opens the door and looks in.

436   EXT./INT.   THE GARAGE, HALLER'S POV   436

LOWE'S coupe is in there. There's just room for it amid the shadowy
piles of bottles and cans.

437   INT.   THE GARAGE, WITH HALLER   437

He goes around to the front of LOWE'S coupe and squats down. In
the b.g.: a heaped mountain of aluminum beer and soda cans.

HALLER feels in his breast pocket and brings out a Zippo. He lights
it and looks at:

438   INT.   THE COUPE, CU   438

One of the turn-signal lenses is broken. There's a scratch in the paint
and a dent in the bumper. HALLER'S fingers come into the frame
and touch the scratch. They stop, and THE CAMERA ZOOMS IN to
a small streak of silvery paint. As MARTY has a scrape of blue car
paint on his wheelchair, so does LOWE have a scrape of silver
wheelchair paint on his car.

439   INT.   HALLER   439

His eyes widen.

SOUND: SHATTERING ROAR and the CLINK AND TUMBLE of
about nine thousand cans as LOWE erupts from under the
aluminum scrap heap behind HALLER. He is a mixture of man and
werewolf, and quite clearly a bestial version of LOWE. In one hand
he holds the remains of ALFIE KNOPFLER'S peacemaker.

HALLER starts to turn; LOWE strikes him with the bat. CAMERA
CLOSES IN ON LOWE as the bat rises and falls . . . rises and falls.
We can't see HALLER, and that is probably a mercy, but we can hear
the THUD of the bat as it strikes again and again and again.

440   EXT.   THE REST AREA AT AUGER FALLS, WITH MARTY, AL,   440
      JANE   DAY

UNCLE AL has taken the Coslaw family station wagon today. The
three of them are sitting in the grove of trees.

                          MARTY
          Mr. Haller said he'd check him out, and guess
          what? No one *sees* him again!

                          UNCLE AL
          And what do you suggest I do about it, dear boy?

MARTY slips off his St. Christopher's medallion and hands it to
UNCLE AL.

                          MARTY
          I want you to turn this into a silver bullet.

                          UNCLE AL
          You're not going to let it go, are you?

                          MARTY
          I saw what I saw.

                          UNCLE AL
          Marty, the moon wasn't even full!

                          JANE (quietly)
          In the made-up stories, the guy who's the werewolf
          only changes when the moon is full. But maybe

he's really that way almost all the time, only as the
moon gets fuller...

MARTY (finishes)
...the guy gets wolfier.

JANE (hands AL her crucifix)
Here. Take mine, too.

MARTY
Jane...you don't have to do that.

JANE
Don't tell me what I have to do and what I don't,
booger-brains.

MARTY
Will you marry me, Jane?

UNCLE AL
Would you kids mind telling me how this guy
Lowe *became* a werewolf to begin with?

JANE
I don't know. Maybe *he* doesn't know, either.

MARTY
No one knows how cancer begins, either, or exactly
what it is—but people still believe in it.

UNCLE AL
The kid is eleven years old and already he sounds
like a Jesuit. A *French* Jesuit.

MARTY
I think he's going to come for me. Not just because
I know who he is, but because I hurt him. Only I
don't think he'll try again as Lowe.

UNCLE AL
Dear boy, you have gone right out of your mind.

MARTY
Will you do it?

UNCLE AL only looks at him, confused and unsure.

441 EXT. A COUNTRY ROAD, WITH THE COSLAW STATION   441
WAGON   DAY

UNCLE AL is taking the kids home—THE CAMERA TRACKS the
wagon for a moment, and then we are looking up the short lane and
into a gravel pit.

THE CAMERA ZOOMS IN, FAST, on the sandy rear wall. We can
see one cowboy boot sticking out of a wall of sand. It's bloody and
chewed.

442 EXT.   THE COSLAW DRIVEWAY   DAY   442

The wagon pulls in.

443 INT.   THE CAR, WITH MARTY, JANE, AND UNCLE AL   443

                        MARTY
Please, Uncle Al.

                        JANE
Will you?

The St. Christopher's medal and the crucifix are hanging from the
rearview on a fine silver chain. UNCLE AL takes down the medal
and looks at it.

                     UNCLE AL
          All right. I give up. Yes.

        MARTY   JANE
All *right*! Thanks!   Thank you, Uncle Al!

                     UNCLE AL
          If either of you ever tells *anyone* I even bought a *piece*
          of this story, werewolves will be the *least* of your prob-
          lems.

444 EXT./INT.   SILVER BULLET MONTAGE   444

    a.) UNCLE AL pulls up to a city store front with a sign reading
        MAC'S GUNS AND AMMO. He takes out the St. Christopher's
        medal, looks at it, and shakes his head, as if still ruing his own
        credulity and stupidity. He goes inside.

                     JANE (voice-over)
          Uncle Al's friend Mac was more than a gunsmith;
          he was, Uncle Al said, an old-world craftsman, a
          sort of wizard of weapons.

    b.) In the gun shop interior, we see UNCLE AL talking to MAC,
        who really *should* look like an elderly white wizard—a kind of
        Gandalf figure. In the b.g. window we see a paper skeleton and
        paper jack-o'-lanterns: our first clue that All Hallows' Eve is
        nearing. UNCLE AL is speaking animatedly, using his hands a
        lot; we don't know exactly what the tale is, but it must be a
        whopper. In the course of it, he hands the medal and the
        crucifix to MAC, who tents the silver chains over his fingers and
        looks at them.

                     JANE (v-o continues)
          God knows what sort of story my uncle told him,
          but I think that for men who have been married as
          often as Uncle Al, invention on short notice
          becomes something of a specialty.

c.) In his workroom, we see MAC spilling boron over the medal and looking closely at the stain.

> JANE (v-o continues)
> The gunsmith confirmed the high-grade silver
> content of my crucifix and Marty's medallion...

d.) In a dim shot which makes MAC look more like a sorcerer than ever, we see him light an acetylene torch and begin melting the medal and the crucifix in the crucible. THE CAMERA MOVES SLOWLY IN as JANE'S contribution and MARTY'S melt together; they are becoming one and indissoluble.

> JANE (v-o continues)
> ...melted them down...

e.) We see MAC pouring molten silver into a bullet mold.

> JANE (v-o concludes)
> ...and molded them into a silver bullet.

445 INT.   MAC'S GUN SHOP, WITH MAC AND UNCLE AL   DAY   445

MAC comes out of the back with small inlaid wooden box. He puts it down on the glass counter top.

> MAC
> Here it is.

446 INT.   THE BOX, CU   446

MAC'S hands open it, disclosing a single bullet resting on dark velvet plush. It is a .22 short round, and it gleams a pure silver. It would be great to hype this bullet optically—not much, just a little—to make it look absolutely magical. Almost holy.

447 INT.   MAC AND UNCLE AL   447

UNCLE AL picks up the bullet almost reverently, holds it to the light.

> MAC
> Nicest piece of work I ever did, I think. It's got a
> low-grain load so it won't tumble. Should be pretty
> accurate.

> UNCLE AL
> It's just a gag, that's all. What would you shoot a
> silver .22 bullet at, anyway?

> MAC (joking)
> How about a werewolf? (Pause) Happy Halloween,
> Al.

243

It nearly fills the screen, swimming mysteriously in the warm
summer air.

> JANE (voice-over)
> By the time Marty's silver bullet was done, it was
> Halloween . . . and the full moon had come around
> again. Earlier that afternoon, my grandfather, who
> had been dying of cancer for over seven years,
> finally finished the job.

THE CAMERA PANS DOWN to the COSLAW house. There's a
carved jack in the window and a corsage of Indian corn on the door.
UNCLE AL'S MG is in the driveway. The COSLAW station wagon is
just backing out. UNCLE AL and JANE stand in the doorway;
MARTY is slightly behind them in the Silver Bullet.

NAN leans out of the car. She's wearing black, and she has
obviously been crying.

> NAN
> Remember, Al . . . we'll be at the Ritz-Carlton in
> Boston tomorrow night! Or at the funeral parlor. It's
> Stickney and—

> UNCLE AL
> —and Babcock, I remember. Now go on!

The station wagon backs farther and NAN leans out again.

> NAN
> And don't you open the door for any trick or
> treaters even if they come!

> UNCLE AL
> We won't!

The station wagon backs out into the road and NAN pops out again.

> NAN
> You kids go to bed on time! You've got school
> tomorrow!

> UNCLE AL
> If you keep doing that, you're going to bump your
> head, sissy. Give my love to Mama—tell her I'll see
> her Thursday.

> NAN
> I will—be good, kids

> MARTY   JANE
> 'Bye, mom! Bye, dad!   We will! 'Bye!

The station wagon accelerates away.

UNCLE AL
Can I tell you kids something?

JANE
Sure, Uncle Al.

UNCLE AL
When me and sissy were kids, we were just like you
two.

MARTY
Yeah? Really?

UNCLE AL
Yeah. Really. The bitch of it is, we still are. Learn from
your elders, dearies.

He ushers them inside and closes the door.

449   INT.   THE STATION WAGON, WITH BOB AND NAN   449

BOB
I can't believe that you'd agree to leave the kids with
him. A year ago I would have laughed at the idea.
You used to almost breathe fire when Al came in the
house.

NAN
He's changed. Just this summer. Or something's
changed him. Marty, maybe. And the drinking . . . I
think it's almost stopped. Whatever it is, it's wonderful. And they'll be safe with him. I'm sure of it.

BOB
I know they'll be safe with him . . . but will he get them
both into bed by nine-thirty?

NAN (firmly)
If I told him to, he will.

450   INT.   THE WALL CLOCK IN THE COSLAW LIVING ROOM   NIGHT   450

It reads 1:00.

SOUND: The National Anthem.

451   INT.   THE TV, CU   451

The anthem finishes up. We go to a station ID card.

ANNOUNCER'S VOICE
This concludes WDML's broadcast day.

The TV goes to snow.

245

452 INT.   JANE ON THE COUCH   452

She's mostly asleep in one corner.

453 INT.   MARTY, IN THE SILVER BULLET   453

He's also dozing.

454 INT.   UNCLE AL, IN BOB'S EASY CHAIR IN FRONT OF THE TV   454

He is also dozing. There are three or four empty beer cans in front of
him, and a cigarette with a long ash is smoldering between his fingers.
There's a .22 pistol in his lap.

455 EXT.   THE COSLAW HOUSE, FROM ONE SIDE   455

The WEREWOLF breaks from the woods and runs across the side yard
to a line of high bushes that runs along the side of the house (this is
the opposite side from MARTY'S bedroom).

456 EXT.   IN THE BUSHES, WITH THE WEREWOLF   456

There is a space in here between the house and the bushes—it's like
an animal's run. The WEREWOLF creeps along this, its one eye flaring.

DIM SOUND of TV SNOW.

457 INT.   THE LIVING ROOM, WITH MARTY, JANE, AND UNCLE   457
AL

UNCLE AL jumps and cries out as the cigarette burns up to his fingers.
The .22 falls onto the rug.

MARTY and JANE also wake up, startled.

458 EXT.   IN THE BUSHES, WITH THE WEREWOLF   458

It recoils, eyes gleaming. Foam begins to drip from its jaws. It creeps
slowly along toward a window. TV SNOW SOUNDS GROW LOUDER.

459 INT.   THE LIVING ROOM, WITH AL, JANE, MARTY   459

UNCLE AL is shaking his burned hand; he picks the cigarette out of
his lap and puts it out.

                    JANE (sleepy)
        You'll burn yourself up sometime doing that, Uncle
        Al.

                    UNCLE AL
        I suppose so. You kids ought to go up to bed.

                    MARTY
        But Uncle Al! You said—

UNCLE AL
I know what I said, Marty—but it's ten past one. He's
not coming.

JANE
The moon's not down yet...

UNCLE AL
Damn near. Now I'll sit up with this stupid gun in
my lap because I promised, but you two are going to
bed. Go on, now, scoot.

JANE gets up and starts toward the stairs.

MARTY
What if I say no?

UNCLE AL
Then I'd have to kick your ass, dear boy. (more kindly)
Go on, now.

MARTY begins to roll the Silver Bullet toward the stairs, where the
stair chair awaits. JANE is waiting for him at the living-room doorway.
MARTY sees the gun on the floor and stops.

MARTY
If that'd gone off, it would have been the end of our
silver bullet.

460 INT.   UNCLE AL   460

He prickles a bit at the unstated criticism. He bends down and picks
up the pistol. He opens the cylinder. Five chambers are empty; in one
there's a bright silver circle.

461 INT.   UNCLE AL   461

He pushes the cylinder plunger, dropping the silver bullet into his hand.

UNCLE AL
See, dear boy? Totally unimpaired.

Behind him, the WEREWOLF'S head appears in the window, its green
eye flaring.

462 INT.   BY THE LIVING ROOM DOORWAY, WITH MARTY AND   462
JANE

MARTY, looking toward UNCLE AL, sees nothing. JANE is looking
toward the window and she SCREAMS.

JANE (shrieking)
*It's him! It's the werewolf! I see him. IT'S THE WERE-
WOLF!*

She's pointing at the window.

247

463 INT.   UNCLE AL   463

He jumps up and looks around at the window—at this point AL has
the .22 with its cylinder open in one hand and the silver bullet loosely
held in the other.

Nothing in the window but darkness. UNCLE AL turns back to the
kids.

UNCLE AL (sharply)
You see it, Marty?

464 INT.   MARTY   464

MARTY (shakes his head)
I was looking at you...

465 INT.   UNCLE AL   465

His shoulders slump a little with relief—now that the scare is over, his
relief is tempered with irritation. They're just a couple of hysterical kids
after all, and JANE is actually worse than MARTY. Polly Practical indeed!

UNCLE AL
A very familiar feeling is beginning to creep over me.

466 INT.   MARTY AND JANE, BY THE DOORWAY   466

JANE is crying.

MARTY
What's that, Uncle Al?

467 INT.   UNCLE AL   467

UNCLE AL
I feel like a horse's ass.

468 INT.   MARTY AND JANE, BY THE DOORWAY   468

JANE (weeping)
I saw it, Uncle Al, I did!

MARTY rolls a little closer to her and attempts to put a comforting arm
around her shoulder.

JANE
Don't you touch me, snotbrains!

MARTY
Jane—

469 INT.   UNCLE AL   469

UNCLE AL
Would you kids go to bed? My head's starting to ache.

470 EXT.   THE SIDE OF THE HOUSE, ECU   470

We see a clawed, hairy hand reach into the frame and close around a
thick wire.

WEREWOLF (voice)
Reeeal slow . . .

It yanks.

471 INT.   THE LIVING ROOM, WIDE   471

The lights go out.

JANE SHRIEKS.

MARTY
It's here! It's outside!

472 INT.   UNCLE AL   472

UNCLE AL
Jane, it's just a power fai—

He's starting toward her. At that moment most of the wall—not just
the window it was looking through before but the whole *wall*—crashes
inward as the WEREWOLF bulls its way through, roaring.

UNCLE AL whirls, raising the pistol automatically to fire—but the
cylinder is rolled out and all the chambers are empty. He has time to
register surprise before the WEREWOLF smashes him aside.

473 INT.   UNCLE AL, A NEW ANGLE   473

He goes flying backward. The pistol goes one way, the silver bullet
another.

474 INT.   THE GUN   474

It spins into a living-room corner.

475 INT.   THE SILVER BULLET, SLOW MOTION   475

We see it rise in the air, turning over and over. It comes down, hits the
floor, and rolls.

476 INT.   THE HALLWAY FLOOR, WITH THE BULLET SLOW   476
MOTION

In the extreme f.g. is a heating vent. The bullet is rolling toward it.

477 INT.   MARTY AND JANE   477

                    MARTY
          Get the gun!

He uses his hands to propel the ungainly Silver Bullet into the hall.

478 INT.   THE BULLET (THE REAL BULLET) AND MARTY SLOW   478
     MOTION

The silver bullet rolls slowly toward the heating vent. In the b.g. we see a frantic MARTY in his wheelchair.

He heaves himself out of it and falls full-length, grabbing.

His fingers touch the bullet, but that's all. It falls in the heating vent.

479 INT.   THE WEREWOLF, CU   479

It's roaring, furious, its one eye flaring.

480 INT.   THE LIVING ROOM, WIDE   480

UNCLE AL lies senseless against one wall, the front of his shirt bloody. JANE runs into the corner and grabs the pistol.

The WEREWOLF picks up the easy chair and throws it through the hole it made coming in. It picks up an end table and hurls it through the TV. Then it sees JANE and starts toward her.

481 INT.   JANE, COWERING IN THE CORNER   481

482 INT.   THE WEREWOLF CU   482

Comes toward her.

483 INT.   JANE IN THE CORNER.   483

She makes as if to run one way.

484 INT.   JANE AND THE WEREWOLF   484

It's only a couple of feet from her now, but again, it is toying with her— it's making this reeeal slow.

485 INT.   THE FIREPLACE TOOLS, CU   485

A bloodstained hand grasps a poker.

486 INT.   THE WEREWOLF AND JANE   486

As it tenses down to leap at her, UNCLE AL leaps at it and strikes it across the back. It turns, ROARING.

UNCLE AL hits it between the legs.

It BELLOWS and grabs the poker. It bends it and tosses it aside. The glaring, savage expression on its face says that now it will bend *UNCLE AL* and toss him aside.

487 INT.   JANE   487

She breaks out of the corner and runs across the room toward the door. Most of the way there she trips and falls.

488 INT.   THE WEREWOLF, CU   488

Its head whips around.

489 INT.   MARTY, IN THE HALL   489

He's lying full-length. He's got the heater vent's grille off. One arm is down inside.

MARTY (screams)
Janey! The gun! THE GUN!

490 INT.   JANE   490

She tosses it awkwardly.

491 INT.   THE GUN, SLOW MOTION   491

It slides down the hall floor to MARTY like some strange, awkward shuffleboard disc, its cylinder still open.

492 INT.   THE WEREWOLF   492

WEREWOLF (snarls)
Maa-aaa-rty . . .

It begins walking slowly across the living room, smashing things out of its way.

493 INT.   MARTY, IN THE HALL   493

The gun slides into his hand. Now he reaches into the heating duct again . . .

494 INT.   IN THE HEATING DUCT, ECU   494

There's an elbow bend just below MARTY'S twisting, grasping fingers—the silver bullet lies here. It's less than half an inch out of reach.

495 INT.   THE WEREWOLF, CU   495

WEREWOLF (foaming)
Maaa-aaa-rty . . .

496 INT.   JANE, ON THE FLOOR   496
                            JANE (sobbing)
                Don't you hurt him! Don't you hurt my brother!

She bites one of the WEREWOLF'S hairy ankles as it passes.

497 INT.   JANE AND THE WEREWOLF   497

It roars with pain and kicks her aside. Then it looks back into the
hall. It is grinning. I believe it is thinking this is going to be better
than a Thanksgiving dinner you don't have to pay for.
                            WEREWOLF
                Reeeal slow, Maa-aaarty—

498 INT.   MARTY, CU   498

He's reaching desperately into the duct and staring at the
approaching WEREWOLF.

499 INT.   IN THE HEATING DUCT, ECU   499

MARTY'S fingers brush the bullet once . . . again . . . seize it.

500 INT.   MARTY, IN THE HALL   500

He rolls over on his back and sticks the silver bullet blindly into one
chamber of the cylinder and slams the cylinder closed.

501 INT.   THE WEREWOLF, CU   501
                            WEREWOLF
                Bastard Marty—

502 INT.   MARTY   502

He points the gun and pulls the trigger. There's only a click. An
expression of dismay on his face.

503 INT.   THE WEREWOLF, CU   503
                            WEREWOLF
                Kill you . . .

504 INT.   MARTY   504

He drags himself so he's half propped against the hall wall. He pulls
the trigger again. Click! Dismay becomes fear.

505 INT.   THE WEREWOLF   505

It's reached the Silver Bullet. It smashes it aside. The Bullet hits the
wall.

506 INT.   MARTY   506

Holding the gun in both hands now, he pulls the trigger a third
time. Click!

The WEREWOLF'S shadow falls over him.

507 INT.   WEREWOLF, ECU   507

WEREWOLF
Bastard Marty!

It bends down, reaching.

508 INT.   MARTY, ECU   508

Cringing back as if to drive himself into the wall, he pulls the trigger
again.

509 INT.   THE BARREL OF THE .22 MAXI-CLOSE   509

The bullet flies from the muzzle, gleaming silver.

510 INT.   THE WEREWOLF   510

The silver bullet strikes him in his one remaining eye. He flies
backward, hands clapped to his gushing face . . . and crashes into
MARTY'S Silver Bullet wheelchair. It sits there, roaring . . . and then
it begins to change.

511 INT.   THE LIVING ROOM FLOOR, WITH JANE   511

She lies there, sobbing.

UNCLE AL (voice)
You okay, Janey?

512 INT.   UNCLE AL AND JANE   512

UNCLE AL is bloody and staggering but on his feet. He helps JANE
up.

JANE
I'm all right . . . but Marty! Ma—

SOUND: SHATTERING ROAR.

513 INT.   THE WEREWOLF, ECU   513

Its hands drop from its face. It is now blind in both eyes; it is half
WEREWOLF and half LOWE.

It BELLOWS again, convulses . . . and dies.

514 INT.   MARTY, ON THE FLOOR   514
                    MARTY (calls)
            I'm all right. He's dead.

515 INT.   UNCLE AL AND JANE   515

        Here's a creature that is mostly FATHER LOWE collapsed in the
        remains of MARTY'S wheelchair; beyond it, MARTY is lying on the
        floor. UNCLE AL goes by the corpse. JANE starts by . . . and LOWE
        sits bolt upright for a moment, grasping blindly at her.

        She shrieks and darts aside. LOWE falls back, now really dead. I
        think. Until the sequel.

516 INT.   THE HALL, WITH UNCLE AL, JANE, AND MARTY   516

        UNCLE AL puts a comforting arm around JANE, who is sobbing
        again—hell, I'd be sobbing after that last one, myself—and draws
        her down beside himself and MARTY.
                    UNCLE AL (to MARTY)
            There. I told you there weren't any such things as
            werewolves.
        They smile at each other with love.
                    JANE (nervous)
            Are you sure it's dead? Or him? Or whatever it is?
                    UNCLE AL
            If it isn't now, it will be after I pound one of your
            mother's silver candlesticks through its heart.
                    JANE (grimaces)
            Oh Uncle Al, no!
                    UNCLE AL (grim)
            Oh yes, Janey. When I believe something, I believe
            it all the way.
        He gets up and leaves.
                    JANE
            Are you all right, Marty?
                    MARTY
            All except my legs . . . I don't think I can walk.
                    JANE
            You're a real booger, you know it?
                    MARTY (smiles)
            I love you, Jane.